ACKNOWLEDGEMENTS

To my baby girl, Rishanna, I love you, and always will unconditionally.

I would like to thank everyone who's important in my life. The list is short, so I won't name anybody. I'm feeling lazy. Just know that I love every single one of you. You should know who you are.

Introduction

Most of us don't realize how lucky we are to be able to wake up everyday without having to worry about whether or not we'll be able to have breakfast, lunch or dinner. We take for granted something as small as a meal because there's an abundance of food available in America.

We often see commercials on television asking for our donation to feed the children of the world, and sometimes we frown upon the idea of even donating ten dollars to help those in need. Unfortunately, hunger is no laughing matter. It can be the difference between life and death for many people who are less fortunate than we are.

Next time you're throwing away food, think about the many children around the world who wish they could have that food to eat. Having had the opportunity to travel outside of the United States, I am grateful that I wake up every morning to find something to eat in my fridge. I'm also grateful that I have available healthcare as well as a decent home to live in.

My experience in Haiti has taught me to appreciate everything that I have in America. From this day on, I pledge not to complain about things that I take for granted, but are considered luxuries to other people. I'm glad also I've had the opportunity to look through the window into some other people's lives who were less fortunate than me. Now, I can confidently say I appreciate my life and I plan to help make the lives of those around me better. Let's take a journey into Haiti…

Welcome to Haiti

Haiti's clear skies, warm sunshine and inviting winds offer the perfect accommodating situation to explore the country's natural splendor. It's undiscovered, pristine trails, and foothills present the best opportunity for a serene bike ride, if that's your thing. An abundance of outdoor opportunities reside in the back mountains of this precious island. The effervescent mood of the people is welcoming and embracing. With plenty of open spaces and green pasture for miles to come, warm climate and plenty of fresh Caribbean air, it's inexcusable to spend too much time indoor on this wonderful island. This aura brought a new sense of being to Deon Campbell. He felt rejuvenated when he first arrived in Haiti.

Deon thought he had left his criminal and troubled past behind and was hoping to start anew in a place where nobody knew his name. The fresh Caribbean air hit his face the minute he stepped off the cruise ship and he just knew that the lifestyle of the rich and infamous was calling his name. With enough money to buy part of the island, Deon wouldn't have any financial worries until his calling from

God in Haiti. On the drive to Jean Paul's mansion, caravan-style, with a Toyota Sequoia ahead of him with armed security men and another Toyota, Land Cruiser truck filled with additional armed security men behind the limousine, Deon's mind was free to think about how he would miss his best friends and buddies, Short Dawg and No neck while riding in the air conditioned, long stretch limousine with his new friend Jean Paul and his entourage. He wanted to exact revenge on the murderers of No Neck and Short Dawg and he would spend as much money as it would take to make sure their killers didn't live to see another day.

"I see you're a serious man, and you're serious about your business," Deon said to Jean Paul as he sipped on a bottle of water while Jean Paul sipped on cognac. "In this country, you have to be. Don't let all the armed security intimidate you, it's a way of life here in Haiti," Jean Paul told him. An additional limousine also followed with all the luggage and money that Deon had to carry to Haiti with him. One of Deon's men rode with the second limousine driver. Keeping his eyes on the prize was very important and Deon didn't hide the fact that he wanted to know where his money was at all times. "I can't help but notice the worried look on your face, your money is fine. I have some of the best security men that Haiti has to offer..." and before the words could escape Jean Paul's mouth, gunfire erupted and bullets were flying everywhere from both sides of the isolated road at a stop sign. A group of men emerged with machine guns and attempted to stop the caravan so they could rob the crew. Deon had been in battle before, but this shit was ten times more than he had ever seen and he didn't know if Jean Paul had set him up or if they were just being robbed. "This fucking Haitian Posse bullshit again!" Jean Paul screamed out loud. "Don't worry about a thing. All the cars are bullet proof down to the tires, but we're gonna teach these bastards a lesson, so they'll never fuck with me again! In each of those little compartments next to the button to lock your door is a nickel plated 9 millimeter, you guys are free to take out as many of them as possible. Their lives are worth shit here," he told them. At the push of a button, Jean Paul opened his compartment and pulled out two loaded .45 Lugar's. He cracked opened his window, and aimed at the pedestrian robbers. The crew of almost 20 men stood no chance as Jean Paul and his men returned fire with high powered guns from the barricaded bullet proof windows of the vehicles. A raid in Vietnam wouldn't even compare to the massacre that went on for about 2 minutes. After all the men were down, Jean Paul got out of the car to make sure that none of them had any breath left in them. It was a killing field as his men went around unloading bullets in the bodies lying across the pavement, ensuring that every single one of them was dead! The last crawling survivor received two bullets in each knee and one to the head before revealing that he was part of the Haitian Posse, located in the slums of Cite Soleil, the most dangerous slum in Port Au Prince, Haiti.

Even the United Nations guards who were sent to monitor the political situation in Haiti were too afraid to go into Cite Soleil. The Haitian police feared confrontation in the slums because they were always outgunned and very few officers who went against the gang lived to tell about it another day. Jean Paul had been a target ever since his arrival in Haiti because of his philanthropic efforts. A reformed, low key former drug dealer who grew up in the States, and was deported back to his homeland some twenty years later, he was not accustomed to the Haitian lifestyle or Haitian culture. After arriving in Haiti, Jean Paul had to learn his culture all over again. Americans like to say they're hungry enough to go do something drastic to feed their family, but in Haiti, those people literally lived it. Forced to eat dirt cookies due to lack of food, money and other resources, these gang members were tired of being hungry and anybody who got in their path paid the price to a better life, or better yet, food.

Many Haitian immigrants left Haiti with the hope to one day go back to their homeland to help with the financial, economical, social infrastructure as well as democratic leadership. However, many of them usually find that what they left behind some twenty to thirty years ago has changed to the worst Haiti that they have ever seen. Since the departure of Baby Doc, Haiti has taken a turn for the worst and the economic climate in Haiti has forced many of its delinquents to become criminals of the worst kinds. While in the United States poor families are offered food stamps, subsidized housing and other economic relief by the government; in Haiti, relief only comes in the form of money sent to those people who have relatives who live abroad. The ones without any relatives, who can afford to care for them financially, suffer the worst kind of inhumane treatment, hunger, malnourishment, social inadequacies and the worst health.

To top off an already problematic situation, many of the Haitian politicians were unconscionable thieves who looked to fill their pockets while the country was in dire need of every imaginable resource possible, including, but not limited to jobs, healthcare, social programs, education, clean water, deforestation, land development, any kind of industry and so on. Many of the elected officials offered promises, but rarely delivered on the promises after taking office. Most of the time, they became puppets of the United States government and in turn, looked for their own self-interest instead of the interest of the people. Deon had no idea what he was stepping into and on the surface it appeared as if he would lead a peaceful life in the first Black republic of the world.

There's a price to be paid for freedom and winning a war against Napoleon's super French army with machetes and pure heart of warriors, the Haitians are definitely paying a price for it now. A brief history on the country was given to Deon and his crew by Jean Paul while on their four-hour drive to Jacmel from Port Au Prince where Jean Paul resided. Deon learned how Haiti, known back then as the pearl of the Antilles, had lost its luster and every resource it used to own due to deforestation. Coffee, sugarcane, cocoa and mangos were just a few of the natural resources and national products that the country used to offer the world, but most of it has evaporated because the government has not provided any assistance to the people to help them become self-sufficient in farming and land development. Security was one of the major reasons why foreign companies stayed out of Haiti, and the government was not doing anything to bring back those companies as well as tourism, which helped the country thrive under the leadership of dirty old Papa Doc.

It was disheartening to Deon and his crew as they watched little kids running wild on the streets digging through piles of trash looking for food, along with the wild pigs and dogs on the side of the roads. Their faces reeked of pain, loneliness, hunger, starvation, malnutrition and hopelessness. Most of them were teary eyed as they watched this for almost two hours during the drive before hitting the scenic part of Haiti. Undeterred by the events that took place in the capital a few hours earlier, Deon ordered the driver to pull over in the center of St. Marc to hand out hundred dollar bills to a group of hungry children. The whole crew took part in handing out the money to the children who looked like they hadn't eaten a good meal since birth. Cindy took it especially hard as she was the only woman amongst the crew and Jean Paul didn't hide the fact that the minority two percent of white people in Haiti and another ten percent of mullatoes and people of mixed heritage controlled the wealth of the nation.

It was evident who the wealthy people in Haiti were as they drove around in their frosty Range Rovers, Land

Cruisers and other big name SUV's with their windows up as they navigated through the ghetto to rape the people of their wealth during the day while they rest their heads in their mansion on the hills at night. The children rejoiced as Deon and the crew gave them enough money that would probably last them a whole month and more, to feed themselves and their families. Jean Paul was happy to see that his new friends sympathized with the people of Haiti, but he cautioned them not to allow their kindness to become a habit because it could be detrimental to their livelihood.

The Run Down

Jean Paul had been in Haiti for nearly two years and he had learned as much as he could about the culture and the political climate of the country. Every crooked politician and police officer was on his payroll. The people, who lived at the bottom of the hill where his house was built, all cherished him because he was the reason why they never went without food. Jean Paul, while he was born in Haiti, was more American than a native born American. His philanthropy in his neighborhood set him apart from all those other people who lived in the big and tall mansions located not too far from his. Jean Paul learned quickly that he couldn't look down upon the common folks like his fellow neighbors. Those people were his watchmen, his lookouts, his security, his peace of mind and his friends. His generosity to them went a long way. Jean Paul tried as much as he could to explain the difference in American culture and Haitian culture to Deon. He affectionately referred to Deon as D. "D, as black people we're naturally selfish because it was forced upon us by the slave-master. We're selfish in the States; we're selfish in Africa, but I have never seen selfishness of this proportion until I got to Haiti. These people are as selfish as they come. 'The crab in the barrel' mentality must've found its inception in Haiti. I have never seen so many people without a social conscience," he said to Deon as the two of them sat in his private office for a little chat after they arrived at his mansion. He was also quick to point out that while many Haitians are selfish towards strangers, they were also the most given when it came to their family. Most of Haiti's people survive on the generosity of family members abroad.

"What's the deal with your peeps, why they seem so selfish, man?" Deon asked with curiosity. "To be honest, I couldn't tell you, man. I am as American as you, because I grew up in the States and my parents pretty much allowed me to live an American lifestyle. However, when I first got here, it was culture shock, man. Nobody wants to help you unless they can benefit from it and there's no such thing as "giving back" to your community, down here. All these rich folks you see up here… have not given a dime back for any kind of park, school or other recreational activities that would benefit the local people who are disadvantaged. These people see me as a god for no reason other than the fact that I spend a few dollars a month to bring smiles to their faces. I have legitimate businesses and I hire many of them, even when I don't need the help, because I know they have to survive. It doesn't take much to live an extravagant lifestyle here, but you have to be careful because everything can be taken away from you at the blink of an eye." Deon just sat there, listened and took everything as a lesson about his new domain. Jean Paul also didn't go into detail about his illegal businesses with Deon either. He would have to wait a few more days to find that out on his own, but that overly lavish lifestyle had to be paid for, some way and somehow.

"Let me ask you something, how does Haitian society function as a whole, I'm talking about what's considered disrespectful here, and some of the Haitian principles and custom that I need to know?" Deon asked. "Well, to be honest, a lot of the Haitian principles won't really apply to you because you are in a better situation than most people in Haiti. You are a millionaire, so everyone will cater to your needs, but it's really up to you to figure out what's disrespectful and what is not, in your interaction with the Haitian people. Most of the people I'm gonna introduce you to, or put you in contact with are just as American as you, so there won't be much to worry about. As far as greeting older people, we usually give the older women, and women in general, a kiss on the cheeks and we slap five with the men, just as you would in the States. It's a learning process and as a hustler who survived MCI Junction at Walpole for twenty years, you'll be fine," Jean Paul told him. "I hope so, man. I think I've already seen a lot during the three hours I've been here on the way from the city. I just hope everything turns out okay," he told Jean Paul reluctantly.

"D, just remember that everything in Haiti has a price on it and be kind to the people who are less fortunate than you. Those are the people who are gonna stand up for you in your darkest hour. Everybody else sees you as a money pit. I'm as brash as they come in Haiti sometimes, but I'm also learning to humble myself. I haven't gotten it quite yet, but I'm working on it. America breeds arrogance and it wasn't until I got here that I learned what it's like to be humble. Over time, I'm sure you will see it the same way. Just be kind to people here and you won't have anything to worry about," Jean Paul advised. "What about that little episode with the gun battle, is that a natural occurrence?" Deon asked. "It is, but you won't have to worry too much about that because my security men will make sure that no one gets close to you. And also, your two new friends, Smith and Wesson, should always be on your waist," he said as he handed Deon two 9-millimeter revolvers. "Your whole crew will be armed and if anybody reaches, don't hesitate to shoot. Welcome to Texas, Cowboy."

Balling Out of Control

Jean Paul was tired of talking about the problems of Haiti and was eager to show Deon and his crew a different side of Haiti, the fun side. After showing the crew their living quarters in this huge mansion where everyone had absolute privacy, Jean Paul wanted to make sure they got a taste of the good life. The good life actually started with the living quarters. Each room was outfitted like a master suite with a bedroom, a living area, walk-in closet and huge bathroom. Four maids were available to the guests twenty four hours a day and two "Gerands," a Haitian term similar to a butler without the tuxedo uniform, but their jobs consisted more of gardening, washing the cars, taking care of the, yard, livestock at the ranch that the maids cooked on a daily basis, and making sure that no uninvited guests sneak onto the property. The funny thing about this little impoverished nation is that people, who can afford it, only eat fresh meat and fish everyday. Everything in Haiti is natural without the added chemical often used in the States to raise livestock and grow food.

The high ceiling, marble floor and arch doorways gave the mansion a feeling of Caribbean royalty. The imported grand scale furniture delivered comfort and luxury; thus, the guests felt welcomed. The thirty-room mansion with maid-quarters, sat on ten acres of land and almost a mile away from the main road. It was total privacy and exclusivity as the cemented rock wall around it gave it a sense of security from any type of invasion. Deon and his crew were impressed, to say the least. Each room was also adorned with a jetted tub and fresh linen delivered daily to the crew as if they were staying at a five-star hotel. Jean Paul was true to his word and he wanted to treat Deon and his crew like royalty.

Everyone went to freshen up before meeting in the grand dining room for dinner. At approximately six o'clock that evening, Jean Paul had his maids and the servers as well as some close friends, at his house for a private party to welcome the crew to Haiti. A dinner amongst a group of fifty friends of Jean Paul's who would also become associates of Deon, should he and Jean Paul ever go into business together. They gathered at the house and the feast lasted almost three hours. Most of the people at the dinner spent half their time in the States and the rest in Haiti. Everybody wanted Deon's ear because Jean Paul had quietly mentioned his financial status as a businessman looking for business opportunities in Haiti. The point was to set Deon up with as many business people as possible to diversify what Jean Paul hoped would be a well-invested portfolio.

On the menu, was the Haitian delicacy called "Lambi," better known as conch meat in English. It's one of the most expensive shellfish in Haiti, equivalent to lobster. The customary rice and beans, chicken, garden salad and the undeniable fried plantains are all part of the Haitian traditional meal and Jean Paul wanted to introduce his new friends to Haitian tradition to the fullest. The twenty servers wore outfits like they were on the bunny ranch. The most beautiful sisters that Jean Paul could find were there to serve the crew. The racy outfits they wore made it hard for Tweak to keep his composure. He was like a kid in a candy store and all the candy was available to him at his request.

Jean Paul also kept caviar flown directly from Russia refrigerated in the stainless steel refrigerator that also kept the hundreds of bottle of "Prestige," the national Haitian beer, Dom Perignon, Moet, Barbancourt Rum, a Haitian favorite, Rum cream and other national alcoholic favorites for the dinner party. However, Deon was only interested in the fresh bottle of Perrier water, as he didn't drink alcohol. His crew partook in all of it. It would take a few days before the crew would get acclimated to the culture of Haiti, but for now, they were just enjoying the ambiance.

Jean Paul

The son of a hard working immigrant couple who worked diligently to bring him to the States as a little boy, Jean Paul's dreams were bigger than his parents' aspiration to continue to clean toilets for a living for the rest of their lives. Two dignified people who believe in hard work and earning a decent living, Jean Paul's parents sought their American dream the best way they knew how. Due to a language barrier, they couldn't use their learned skills to provide for their son. His dad was a farmer and his mom was a cook who originated from a small town in Haiti called St. Louis Du Sud. After they arrived to the United States from Haiti, they struggled because they couldn't understand English. Since French is the official language in Haiti, the transition to learn English kept the couple from getting decent job offers, so they had to do what was necessary to care for their child that they left back in Haiti with his grandmother. Their survival instinct kicked in when they realized that they had extra mouths to feed back home. The easiest jobs for immigrants to find in the United States are the ones that Americans are less likely to accept in the housekeeping field. Jean Paul's mother worked as a housekeeper at a local hotel while his father worked as a janitor at a hospital.

Jean Paul's parents had to pay a lot of money to get a visa to come to the States as visitors. It was while they were in the United States visiting that they made the decision to stay permanently. Their visa also didn't allow them to work in America, which was one of the reasons that they struggled so much. It wasn't until they were granted amnesty a few years later that they were able to receive a decent wage. Their main goal was to bring their son to America as quickly as they could, and that happened a year after they received their Green cards and permanent alien resident status. Jean Paul's parents worked long hours and barely made enough money to survive. His parents looked a lot older than their actual age from hard work. Jean Paul couldn't see himself fitting that lifestyle. Jean Paul's decision to become a drug dealer was made easy by the local hustlers on his block who paraded around in BMW's and Mercedes Benzes all day. The hustlers never discussed the end results with Jean Paul; they only allowed him to see the flashy side of hustling, but not the hustle and bustle and the possibilities of jail and death.

As a young man, Jean Paul was often left alone in the house while his parents worked long hours to support him and their extended family back in Haiti. It didn't take long for him to figure out his parents' schedule and started wandering off in the hood to hang with the big boys.

Armed with the vigor and determination to become one of the most successful drug dealers in Boston, Jean Paul set out to work for one of the top guys coming up in the drug game in his hood. As a twelve year-old, Jean Paul was smarter than most kids. The older rock slingers on the block made sure he handled every transaction with new customers. Jean Paul was always smart enough to ask the customers if they were cops before handing any drugs over to them. At first, he wasn't gaining much. The guys would offer to buy him clothes and sneakers but he knew better not to bring those items home as his parents would beat the silliness out of him. He opted for the money instead. He continued to wear the K-Mart brand clothing and shoes that his parents bought him while stacking his paper. Jean Paul also used leave money in his parents' path on purpose as if God was mysteriously blessing them with money on the ground.

By the time he turned fifteen years old, he had grown to be 5ft 10 inches tall with a considerable amount of weight at 150 pounds for his age, and his dark complexion and infectious smile made him appear innocent. He had earned the trust of his parents due primarily to the fact that he was a good student at school. Jean Paul was also a tough little boy who used to take on the other boys in the school yard. Those fights were usually arranged by the older guys on the block. He had gained the reputation of a pit-bull as a fighter. His parents never knew of his street dealings and when he told them he wanted to get a part-time job, they were more than open to the idea.

Jean Paul took on a part-time job at the local supermarket that lasted a couple of weeks. He was able to show his parents his paycheck and they trusted that he was becoming a responsible young man. They continued to work long hours and spent very little time with him. They wanted to secure his future for college and the home they had to scrape money to pay for every month. Meanwhile, Jean Paul saw the fast money on the street started to quadruple. It was because of that reason he stopped working at the supermarket. He dealt weed and crack on the street while keeping up with his grades at school. He was leading a double life. For years, Jean Paul never had any encounter with the police about his drug deals. He was also absorbing everything about the game. As he moved up in ranks on the street, he started paying off cops that he knew were more than just too happy to make an extra grand every week. Keeping "Popo" off his trail was essential to his success. Netting close to fifty thousand dollars a week, Jean Paul knew that the authorities had to be paid off. There was no where to go but up and he was on his way to earn millions of dollars in the game.

The money was coming in fast and in bundles. Jean Paul had guys in almost every corner pushing his signature crack to the folks in the hood by the time he was a senior in high school. His main supplier was in the Springfield, Massachusetts area and he would drive down to Springfield once a week to pick up his supplies. After his dad helped him get his license, he went and bought a black Volkswagen, GTI. The car was equipped with every accessory imaginable, making Jean Paul an easy target for the feds and the cops. However, Jean Paul had the gift of gabs. The few times he was pulled over by the cops while driving, he was clean as a whistle. He also didn't use his personal car to make his run. He used to pay this older guy to rent him a car, so he could go to Springfield on his runs.

By the time Jean Paul graduated from high school, he had already gotten his own place while his parents thought he was living on some campus somewhere. He did enroll at a local university in Boston to study business. Jean

Paul looked like he came from an affluent family on campus. He wore the latest fashion and sported some of the most expensive jewelry. Many of the students at the school had no idea about his background. Jean Paul was also intelligent in class. He challenged his teachers and questions facts and theories presented to him in class. Trying to navigate the streets and balancing school would prove challenging at times for Jean Paul, but he was focused and determined. He was going to accomplish his goals in spite of the hurdles he faced.

Jean Paul also had to become more ruthless with his dealings on the street by the day. His nemesis wanted to test his strength and heart. While Jean Paul showed a great deal of concern about his livelihood and his stance in society, he also understood that all of it could be taken away from him in a flash. He became the victim of a robbery when one of his adversaries caught him coming out of a store on Blue Hill Avenue one evening. "Kick in your chain or get your head blown off, mothafucka," said the man holding the 9mm automatic glock revolver to Jean Paul's head, while his accomplice looked on. Contemplating his next move, Jean Paul knew that he had no chance against the two stick-up kids when he noticed a chrome .45 around the other guy's waist. Reaching for his own weapon would be deadly at this point. "You're gonna have to snatch it, if you really want it, bruh," he said to the man. "Have it your way, motherfucka," the man said while snatching the platinum chain with the diamond piece from Jean Paul's neck. "And while you're at it, empty your pocket, too, motherfucka!" the robber ordered. Jean Paul complied and gave up his money. He also noticed a distinctive tattoo on the robber's right hand that was all too familiar.

The stick-up kids took off down the street before Jean Paul had a chance to retaliate, but he had a plan. Jean Paul already knew who the stick-up kids were. The tattoo on the kid's arm identified him as Sean, a member of a rival drug crew from Heath Street project in Jamaica Plain. Jean Paul lost a cool ten G's in cash and twenty thousand dollars worth of jewelry from that little incident. He knew he couldn't let that go, or he would become a target for all the stick-up kids in Boston trying to make a name for themselves on the street. Before word could get around that he had been robbed, Jean Paul went home and put together a plan to make the robbers pay. He knew exactly where to find them. At first, Jean Paul wanted to take care of it alone; then he thought about a possible ambush in the event that the robbers were waiting for him. There was only one person that he could trust with his life, and that person was none other than, Diggy, Crazy D's cousin.

Outfitted with black jeans, boots, hoodies, dark sunglasses, silencers, Tech 9's and automatic Tech 9 Uzi machine gun, Jean Paul and Diggy set out to find the stick-up kids while driving a hot box. Back then, they referred to stolen cars as hot box in the hood in Boston. The Mustang GT pulled up slowly on a corner side street near Heath Street project where the two robbers posted to sling their rocks to the ever-growing population of desperate crackheads sprouting up all over the projects looking for a way to deal with their everyday problems. One of them was bold enough to wear the chain around his neck like he was on some Nino Brown shit from New Jack City, while his partner stood beside him like Tony Montana in Scarface, replaying the whole event about the robbery to their crew. Unfortunately, neither Nino Brown nor Tony Montana ever let their guards down like that. As the black mustang crept up, Jean Paul could see the bling from his diamond piece almost a block away as it shined while the street light caressed it. "That's dem motherfuckas right there rocking my chain. We're smoking all of them," he said to Diggy. Diggy was known around Boston as one of the best getaway drivers to ever live. During police chases around Boston,

Diggy always managed to evade capture by the police behind the wheel of a car, any car. There was no arguing who was going to be behind the wheel as they set in motion their plan for revenge.

Jean Paul tightened the silencer on his automatic Tech 9 Uzi to make sure everything was okay. Diggy kept his Tech 9s close to him, one on his lap and the other in his right hand, while riding down the street full speed before they came to a halt in front of the crowd of men who gathered on Jean Paul's side of the street. The Mustang GT careened to a stop as Diggy and Jean Paul jumped out of the car to unload their automatic weapons on the crowd of young men. People were running like wild roaches when gunfire erupted from left and right. Jean Paul unloaded his Uzi, hitting at least four of the men, including the one who was sporting his chain, while Diggy was strictly aiming for people's domes killing all three of the men he hit instantly. Two people from the crew were able to escape with wounds to their legs while the rest lay in a pool of blood breathing a mixture of mucus and blood before their hearts gave up. Jean Paul snatched his chain back and the money from the kid's pocket before he hopped back in the hotbox burning rubbers down the street, heading to their side of the hood.

The streets were hot for weeks to come. Jean Paul knew that he and Diggy had to lay low for a while. Even though they were wearing hoodies and sunglasses that barely allowed a glimpse into their identities, the other crew pretty much figured who the culprits were. They hadn't thought their retaliation through long enough. Every hustler in Boston knew that Diggy was Jean Paul's right hand man, and that the two of them were in it to win it. Now they were on the other crew's hot list of wanted men.

Jean Paul told Diggy that they needed to lay low for a while. He even suggested that they'd go to Atlantic City to let things cool down, but Diggy saw it as a sucker move. He wasn't afraid of anybody and he didn't care about the chumps that he shot because they had robbed his boy. Most people on the street already knew that Diggy was trigger happy and he feared no one. His reputation preceded him as a true gangster. However, no matter hard a gangster thinks he is; it only takes one bullet to take him out. Diggy got caught off guard one day when one of his enemies saw him walking out of a sub shop down Dudley station. He had a thing for steak-n-cheese subs and he couldn't go a day without eating one. Just as he was about to walk to his car with a sub in hand, the gun shots rang out. Diggy had left his gun in his car while picking up the sub and had no weapon to defend himself. He dodged behind a car for cover, while the sub fell out of his hand and hit the ground. It was a single shooter and he continued to pursue Diggy as he rolled around on the ground behind the car. A few more shots rang out and suddenly Diggy's blood started streaming down on the pavement from behind the car. The shooter knew that he had hit his target. He hopped in a car and took off. By the time the paramedics responded, Diggy was resting in peace in gangster heaven, if there was such a place.

When Jean Paul got word of Diggy's death, he knew that there was going to be a lot of bloodshed in Boston that summer. One by one, he started taking out the crew he suspected murdered his friend. By the time summer was over Jean Paul had decimated enough members and instilled enough fear to force that crew to dissipate. Unforeseen throughout his crew, was a snitch who gave up Jean Paul for a couple of the murders of the other crew's members to save his ass when the feds locked in on him. One of Jean Paul's soldiers sold him out to the feds to keep a lifetime sentence short. Jean Paul never saw it coming when he stepped into court with his expensive lawyer who had no idea that the feds had caught themselves a snitch who agreed to testify that he saw Jean Paul pull the trigger at least twice to kill two men. By the end of trial, Jean Paul was sentenced to life in prison, but because he wasn't a US citizen, he was deported back to his homeland a few years later to make room at the prison to accommodate more prisoners. Unfortunately, the snitch who sold him out is now getting around in a wheelchair while he's totally incapacitated. He was sodomized with a broomstick that hit his spinal cord while in jail and no one ever found out who did it.

It had taken five years for the state to bring the indictments against Jean Paul. In the meantime, he had amassed enough wealth to live comfortably for the rest of his life. The prosecutor was even shocked when Jean Paul showed up in court with the highest paid attorney known in the Commonwealth of Massachusetts. They wondered how much money this man really had. Jean Paul couldn't keep from shining. He liked nice things and he lived his life luxuriously in the public's eyes. The day that brought his downfall in court was not foreseen by him or his high priced attorney. He was so confident that he was gonna walk, he didn't even make the proper arrangements for life behind bars. He was just whisked away and had to do all his planning in a 10X10 jail cell.

Jean Paul learned many lessons while he was hustling on the street, but the most important lesson he learned was that many people in the game aren't cut out for the game. Bitches and snitches come a dime and dozen and the game is not immune to them. Ever since then, he had been very careful with the company he kept. And even in jail he was a loner until he met Crazy D and his crew. Jean Paul had served almost seven years in prison before the State Department decided to ship him back to Haiti. He knew once he touched down in Haiti, there was nothing but the good life waiting for him. His wife had proven to be trust worthy, so he thought.

Jean Paul had also learned that he should always take care of those who take care of him. Reaching out to Deon was the natural thing to do after Jean Paul got settled in Haiti. He also knew that Deon and his crew would be a great investment for Haiti with all the money that they were bringing down with them. He wanted to see them prosper peacefully and be a good host for as long as they needed him to be. That was his good karma. Jean Paul more than anything wanted to make sure his family was provided for and be a good enough husband to his wife. However, things don't always go as planned.

For most Haitian men in Haiti, being a good husband simply means that he's a good provider who takes good financial care of his family at home. Many of them act like single men and still go out and play. Many Haitian men in Haiti have more than one woman and most of the time the wife knows about it. It's rare that some of them don't have kids with other women while married to their wives. And the wives seldom leave their husbands even after the revelation of an affair or love child or children from other women. Jean Paul was no different. He conveniently picked and chose the American customs that he wanted to maintain after moving to Haiti, and being unfaithful was a Haitian custom he was not willing to give up. Since Jean Paul's second love was women, he figured he might as well shower his guests with some of the most beautiful women Haiti had to offer. Crazy D and his crew would have the time of their lives with these women.

Deon, Cindy and Maribel

Crazy D found out a wild side to Cindy that he hadn't been privy to. Cindy was more than willing to have her coochie licked by a few of the women in the house. She couldn't help being attracted to a couple of them. Maribel was a stunning beauty from the Dominican Republic. Crazy D couldn't believe it when he first laid eyes on her. She was specifically instructed by Jean Paul to take care of Crazy D and no one else. Jean Paul was not yet clear on whether or not Crazy D and Cindy was a couple. He wanted to make sure the man was taken care of. Standing at 5ft 8 inches tall, with thirty-four D cup sizes, a waist so small that Crazy D could wrap one hand around it, and booty so nice and round that J-Lo would have to get surgery to be that perfect, Maribel was the bomb. The tempted grin on Crazy D's face was read by Maribel almost instantly. Always the trooper, Cindy also noticed the grin on Crazy D's face as she suggested they take her to the room for a threesome. "I can see it in your eyes. You wanna fuck the hell out of her," Cindy told Crazy D. He smiled because he knew she was right.

Though she couldn't speak a lick of English, Maribel could read Crazy D's body language and she knew that he wanted a piece of her. "Don't worry, I want her too. It's been a while since I've had a beautiful woman," Cindy revealed. Crazy D shook his head in amazement and said nothing. "I know I never told you that I was bisexual, but it's one of the perks that you'll have by being with me. You can always have the woman of your choice, as long as I have some of her as well," Cindy revealed to him. No man in his right mind could pass up on that kind of deal, and Crazy D was the player of all players. That's the type of chick he wanted. He knew he wasn't the one-woman kind of man. Crazy D, however, hadn't started to fall for Cindy the way she had fallen for him.

As Maribel walked up the stairs in front of Cindy and Crazy D to head to the room, Cindy palmed her ass. Maribel looked back and smiled at the gesture. Crazy D was just thinking about how he was going to fuck the hell out of both women. Crazy D's ten-inch snake was starting to unfold and by the time he reached the door to the master suite, he was unfastening his belt because he wanted Maribel and Cindy to get on their knees and start slobbing on the knob simultaneously. Maribel was a complete sexual kitten. She had sexy brown eyes and long curly black hair that flowed down her back. She reached for Crazy D's long, hard and delicious dick, and wet her whistle. She wanted to blow the hell out of him. Cindy held her hair back from her face as Deon's dick found the back of her throat moment later. She kept sucking on the head while she looked up at him to see his reaction. "Yeah, suck it. Suck that dick with yo fine ass," Deon told her. Though she didn't understand what he said, she knew to keep sucking his dick with as much fervor as ever. The shifting of her head from left to right offered Deon a sexy view of her profile. This chick was fine from every angle.

As Deon stood there enjoying Maribel's lips around his dick, he urged Cindy to get involved. Cindy let go of Maribel's hair and grabbed the base of Deon's ten-inch hardened dick so Maribel could focus on sucking instead of holding it. And then Cindy couldn't hold back any longer. She took her lips and placed it on the shaft of Deon's dick as Maribel licked the base. The two tongues started to intertwine at the tip of Deon's dick. Deon stood in the middle grabbing a hand full of hair on both sides as the two women had a dick sandwich in their mouths. Both were vying for more reaction from Deon. The more fierce they got with their tongue, the louder Deon's growls became. "I want you to suck her titties," Deon said to Cindy while

Maribel continued to suck his dick. Cindy was sucking Maribel's titties while rubbing her clit with her finger. The moaning and groaning was serious as Deon reached over to stick his middle finger in Cindy's ass. She loved getting stuck in the ass, and Deon always obliged her.

The three of them moved over to the oversized couch, located in the adjacent open space to the bed. Deon wrapped himself in a condom while Maribel straddled him. Cindy stood at the head of the couch with her leg raised against the back part of the couch above Deon with her pinkness spread across his face. Deon's tongue strokes were lethal. He had become an expert pussy-eater through practice with Cindy. She couldn't keep her composure as her wet pussy was being devoured with strokes, after strokes, after strokes by Deon. Meanwhile, Maribel was enjoying the ride as she mounted Deon's ten inches. The back and forth thrusting on Deon's dick was something that Maribel had never experienced. She was enjoying it so much she could hardly keep her eyes open. It was the same for Deon as he felt her round booty on his pelvis and the soothing comfort of her warm pussy enfolded his dick. Heaven was near, but Deon was trying hard to fight it. Cindy took notice almost immediately. How was she going to keep this black man happy with so very little booty? She thought. Deon had never been a slave to booty or beauty, but Maribel wasn't exactly your everyday beauty nor did she carry your everyday, average booty. She was as gorgeous as they came and Cindy had better start playing her position.

Always the oral expert, Cindy decided to play her strength. Before Deon could reach the gates of heaven inside Maribel, Cindy told him, "I want you to come in my mouth, baby." Deon already knew that Cindy had enough skills with her tongue to make him cum, and the idea of her swallowing a couple of tablespoon of protein down her throat without flinching was very appealing to him. Maribel dismounted Deon and Cindy pulled the condom off Deon's dick and commenced her tongue attack on his dick. Round and round she went with her tongue while using her free hand to massage the base of Deon's balls. All Maribel could do was stand back and watch the oral expert performed while she took Deon to the promise land. Maribel took it up a notch as she leaned down and squeezed every last drop of sperm out of Deon's dick into Cindy's mouth. She wasn't much for tasting cum, but with the competition having the upper hand, she decided to partake in the cum-shake, as she took about half a teaspoon down her throat as well.

Satisfied with his nut, Deon turned on the television while he lay in bed with the two women. Later on, they would put on a show for him that he had never in his life seen before. Maribel and Cindy would fuck each other until they both came all over one another. Deon thought long and hard about keeping Maribel around. It was a decision that he couldn't fight. Her beauty alone was enough to make any man go crazy. Coupled with her body, Maribel was going to be around for a while.

Tweak and Nadege

For the first couple of weeks, Crazy D and his crew had nothing but fun in Haiti. Jean Paul made sure they were entertained like stars. They toured almost the entire country and Jean Paul made sure they saw Haiti for what it really was, a place where anybody could live in obscurity as long as they were law-abiding citizens and didn't meddle in other people's business, as well as a place where one could easily become a target and be taken out without a second thought. Jacmel was a beautiful place to be but Deon and the crew had yet to see the best parts of Haiti. Jean Paul arranged a tour of Cap Haitien so the crew could visit the Citadel. One of the biggest fortresses in the world built by black men with the mortar-mix made mostly of the French soldiers' blood. The Citadel should have been the eighth wonder of the world because of the architecture alone. They also went to the Sans Souci palace, one of the biggest palaces in Haiti. Other beautiful cities and towns like Les Cayes, Miragoane, Gonaives, Petit Trou De Nipe, Iles De La Tortue and many other beautiful serene parts of Haiti.

Deon, Tweak, Smitty and Crusher also got more pussy during those two weeks than they had ever had their entire lives. It was the crème de la crème as far as the kind of women Jean Paul brought to the house to entertain them. The guys had never had a real vacation where they simply sat back and enjoy life. This was the first time that they were able to go to the white sand beaches of Haiti escorted with the finest women Haiti had to offer. Though pussy was never a problem in the States for these guys, they never took their time to really enjoy any of it. Jean Paul was about to change their pussy experience and the fellas couldn't believe their eyes when they saw these women.

Tweak was like a kid in a candy store. Since he was more on the scrawny side, he wanted a woman with meat on her bones. Nadege was a full figured, stunning beauty straight from Cap Haitien, which is located on the northern part of Haiti. Cap Haitien is the second largest city in Haiti, but that city also boasts some of the most beautiful women that the country has to offer. His mouth was watering as he entrenched himself in Nadege's natural beauty. Her long flowing hair, big eyes and beautiful smile had Tweak hooked from the very start. He didn't dare try a threesome because Nadege was more than enough woman for him. She stood at 5ft10 inches at about two-hundred and fifteen pounds, with the weight evenly distributed to all the right places. Ass was booming like a Blaupunkt speaker and her 38 DD breasts took over half of her torso. Nadege made "Buffy 'the Body'" look anorexic. As thick as Nadege was, her stomach was as flat as an ironing board with hips expanded all the way to the States. Tweak couldn't wait to jump her bones. Nadege only knew a few words in English, but those few words would go a long way with Tweak. "What you like?" she asked Tweak in a sexy Haitian accent that Tweak had never heard before. She was also a little shy, which brought about the kind of excitement that a man like Tweak would enjoy since he was shy himself. "I like licky licky," Tweak said to Nadege while pointing to his dick like she was Asian or some shit. "Oh, you like blowjob," she said. "Yes, yes I love blowjobs. Blowjobs all day for me," Tweak said excitely.

  Nadege sensually made her way down to Tweak's crotch and commenced to unfasten his belt. She almost choked on her own saliva when she noticed skinny ass Tweak's twelve-inch dick. She never thought a dude that skinny could have such a fat dick, and to top it off, Tweak didn't even look like a guy who was packing. "Oh my God," she whispered as she took his dick in her hand. "You like?" he asked. "Dangerous," she responded while holding in her fear. "Are you gonna keep rapping on the mic or am I gonna get some licky licky action here?" Tweak asked impatiently, while Nadege was still admiring his dick in shock. "I suck now," she said. She took his dick in her mouth and started doing tricks with her tongue that Tweak had never experienced before. She had a mouth full as she jerked his dick back and forth with her tongue wrapped tight on the head. Tweak took a hold of the back of her head and slowly started to hump her mouth. He was trying his best to be gentle but Nadege was a whole lot of woman and Tweak was eager. 'I wanna fuck your big ass titties," he said. "Fuck titties, how?" she asked. You mean to tell me no man ain't never fucked them big ass titties befo? Let me show you. Tweak sat Nadege on the edge of the bed, while he grabbed her titties with both hands placing his dick in the middle. He held her titties tight together while he humped her. His dick was so long, she was able to catch the head in her mouth with each hump. "I wanna suck them titties too,'" he told her. He dropped to his knees as he allowed one of her tits to cover half his face while sucking on the other one. Tweak took the oversized nipple in his mouth and started to gently suck on it. "Suck hard, baby," she directed him. He added more pressure to his suction and Nadege started to lose control. "Ouh! Cheri ou dous," she said in her native tongue.

Tweak didn't understand what the hell she said, but the sound of her tone was so sexy, he wanted to hear more. He moved on to the other breast while he continued to play with one with his hand. The harder he sucked, the tighter her grip on the bed became. "Taye'm Cheri!" She screamed. "What?" he asked confusingly. "I mean fuck me, baby," she said after Tweak almost made her cum while sucking her titties. He wrapped himself in an extra large Trojan condom before entering Nadege's dripping pussy.

He kept her ass close to the edge of the bed while holding her legs apart exposing the pinkness of her fat pussy to his hungry dick. He slowly inserted his dick and she started wincing as the inches increased. After Tweak got about a good ten inches inside her, he started to slowly stroke her. "Dick is big and good!" she yelled at the top of her lung while his skinny ass stroked away. Tweak wanted to get to her wall and he couldn't help himself as he stroked all twelve inches inside her "Amwey!!!!" she screamed in her native tongue in pleasure. Tweak was a little confused. "You want me to stop?" he asked. "No, it's very good," she said. He kept stroking her, but the weight of her legs on his arm was starting to take its toll. He brought her down to the edge of the bed so he could fuck her from the back. Nadege had enough ass to share with enough white women in any

Midwestern town, USA with flat asses. Tweak grabbed hold of her ass cheeks and started beating her pussy with his dick. The harder he fucked her, the more she wanted. She decided to just lay her torso flat on the bed with her ass sticking up while Tweak fucked her until she started shaking. "Map voye! Cheri, map voye!" she started screaming in her native tongue again. Her body couldn't stop shaking as Tweak made her cum over and over until he released his own nut in the middle of her crack, after pulling off the condom. Sweat was pouring down their bodies as they both lay on the bed for a quick rest before Tweak got up again for round two.

Nadege had never been fucked like that before. She was shocked and awed to discover what the skinny man with the big dick was capable of. Her pussy would get wet every time she thought about Tweak.

Nadege came from a poor family where they had just the basic necessities to survive. Her father was a farmer or "planter" as they are called in Haiti. He had four children with his wife, but old age and illnesses forced him into early retirement. When he could no longer work the field to provide for his family, his beautiful daughter decided she would do her part to help take care of her parents and her sibblings. Nadege met Jean Paul while he was visiting Cap

Haitien. She had just finished high school, but there was no opportunity for her to get a job in her city. He thought her northern accent was funny when he first met her. She didn't sound like she was from the city and that appealed to him. She wanted to go on to school to study medicine, but her family didn't have the money to pay for her schooling. Jean Paul was trying to figure out what kind of job he could offer Nadege. Though she wasn't exactly his type of woman, her beauty couldn't be denied. Jean Paul didn't need a maid or servant; he had enough of those already. He figured he could use Nadege as his personal secretary. When Nadege saw Tweak, it was almost love at first sight. His light brown skinny frame appealed to her dark chocolate healthy frame. The night they spent together that night broke down the language barrier that would prevent them from falling for each other. Tweak was definitely not a player. He was more of a one woman type of man. Nadege was all the woman that he ever needed.

Crusher and His Women

Crusher's big ass couldn't handle the two women he took to his room with him. Crusher looked like a giant compared to the two tiny women he took to the room with him. Evelyne was a light skinned Jacmel native. The natives refer to her as a "grimelle," because of her light complexion. She was one of the chicks that Jean Paul hired to just be around. Whenever he went out, she was one of the dimes on his arms. Of course, he had slept with every dime in that house, except for Nadege. However, Jean Paul was also a very unattached man. He was like a pimp, without having his women work the street to earn him money. Crusher's bicep was an amazement to Evelyne. That huge black American was a foreign thought to her. She had never traveled to the States, so she thought that America was only made up of white people. She tested him to see if he could speak Creole, but Crusher never responded to her comments. Finally, she accepted the fact that he was a black American and she was ready to taste some of his American dick.

The other woman that he picked was a dark skinned sister straight from the capital city in Cite Soleil, a place she often visited whenever she had a chance. She was a little more bright eyed and experienced than the other girls. She knew that because Crusher was American he automatically had money and he could also be her ticket out of Haiti. Her intent from the very beginning was to get him hooked. She had been fucking Jean Paul for a while, but she knew nothing serious was ever going to become of her position with him, even though she was loyal to him to death. He had a wife. Her name was Rosie. She had bigger dreams than just being Jean Paul's boy toy. Though he gave the women an allowance of $500.00 US dollars a month plus room and board, which was a very attractive salary in Haiti, she knew that her youth would eventually fade along with her beauty and she would have to create a better life for herself. Unlike, the rest of the women, Rosie was only responsible for herself as she had no family that she knew of. Both of her parents died when she was a child and one of her aunts sold her into servitude when she was six years old. She became a "Restavek," which is close to what most people in the States would consider a child slave. Rosie's tumultuous, pain-filled life ironically was not so rosy at all. Forced to work almost 18 hours a day, Rosie never had a chance to go to school to learn how to read and write. She was very domesticated and was also a sex slaves by the time she turned ten years old. The couple she was sold to, used and abused her in every way possible. Though these people could barely afford to provide for themselves, the standard of living in Haiti is so low, pretty much anyone with an extra dollar a month could afford to have a child slave, thus, Rosie was brought in.

A country with no child labor laws and protective service for children, Haiti is the Mecca of child slavery. The Haitian government does very little to ensure the safety of the homeless children in the streets. At any moment they can be beaten, raped arrested, ridiculed and even killed without any ramification. The lawlessness in Haiti has forced the country to prioritize more important issues like, the politicians robbing the country of its wealth. In the United States, the president has a set salary that is determined by the federal government. However, in Haiti, most of the country's wealth is the president's salary. By the time they leave office or get chased out by the people, they are multi-millionaires.

As a child, Rosie's days consisted of getting water from the local reservoir, carrying a 30-gallon bucket on her head for almost a mile on her tiny frame; going to the local market daily to buy whatever was needed to cook the daily meal, washing everybody's clothes, sweeping and mopping the house, and washing the dishes at night before she goes to sleep on the cold floor in the tiny front room the family called a living room. She would throw a couple of pieces of rags on the floor to serve as cushion between her body and the cold cement floor. She was also the first person up every morning to make coffee for the family and to make sure the couple's children, who were much older than her, were ready for school.

By the time Rosie reached ten years old, the molestation at the hand of the woman's husband began. Her developing breasts became his toy whenever his wife was not around. It was like he was just waiting for her to reach puberty. When she finally did, the fondling of the breasts escalated to full blown sex. Eleven-year-old Rosie had to have sex with this sick man almost everyday, or he threatened to kick her at the house. By the age of twelve, Rosie had become somewhat of an expert in what the man liked, but his sixteen year old son also wanted in on the action as well. He threatened to tell his mother that she was stealing if she didn't have sex with him. She was left with no choice. Rosie wasn't just getting abused sexually, she was also beaten on a daily basis by the wife whenever the wife thought she did something wrong. By the time she turned fourteen years old, she had had enough. Rosie decided to run away and never came back. She met a woman who was a former "Restavek" who claimed she wanted to help her, but the woman turned out to be just as abusive. Rosie lasted less than three years at the woman's shack before she decided to run away again.

Meanwhile, Rosie's natural beauty was slowly emerging. Though she was poor and couldn't afford to maintain herself, Rosie had a natural glow about her. She had decided to save her money while she was living with the woman who also sold her into prostitution. She would perform extra favors for guys to get extra money without the woman's knowledge. She had become an oral expert and words got around that she was the best at what she did. Men used to come looking for her just to sample the goods, and Rosie always delivered. She used the money she saved to get her own business started at 'Marche Fer," which was the local market where people went shopping everyday for fresh meat, produce and vegetables. Rosie invested all of her money into fruits and vegetables and she started selling them everyday at the market. She would do this for three years until she made enough money to enroll in school at night. All Rosie ever wanted to do was to learn how to read and write. She was able to enroll in school at night to learn the basics of reading, writing and arithmetic. Rosie also started taking better care of herself. She started buying second hand clothes brought to Haiti by merchants in bulk purchased from Goodwill and other thrift stores in the States. The clothes known as "Kennedy or Pepe," were usually sold at the market for pennies on the dollar. Rosie was wearing the hell out of a pair of used Calvin Klein jeans when Jean Paul ran into her on her way home from school. She had grown to be a very curvaceous and beautiful young woman. Jean Paul could see the beauty hidden under the sadness that was written on her face. She was very cordial when he approached her from his SUV. He soon started to pick her up from school to take her out to eat. She was always too ashamed to take him to the little shack where she lived, so he ended up spending time with her at the local hotel before he went home to his wife. She also knew about his wife because he told her from the very beginning. Rosie saw an opportunity for a better life from Jean Paul and she seized it. When he asked to move her to Jacmel, she didn't hesitate to accept his offer with one stipulation; she would continue to go to school. Rosie was a sexpert and Jean Paul couldn't get enough of her. She was his favorite girl for a while until he met another gorgeous woman who started to occupy most of his time. Rosie played her position and allowed Jean Paul to be who he was.

Smitty

While everyone was smashing the available, bodacious ladies at the mansion, young Smitty had his mind set on his money and his money on his mind. He came to Haiti as a soldier in The Hoodfellas organization, but he intended to become a general in no time. He had been watching Jean Paul and Deon's interactions and from that, he knew he wanted to be a boss some day. He was not the underling type and he was gonna show and prove to Deon that he was a worthy protégé. Smitty was like a sponge, absorbing everything that Deon dished out. He even tried to capture Deon's swagger and developed his own in the process to fit the mold of a bossman. Though he didn't want to be a clone of Deon, he admired the man like Kobe admired Michael Jordan as a young player when he first came to the NBA league. Deon hadn't spent much time schooling the youngster since they arrived in Haiti, but he did give him encouraging words everyday to make sure that Smitty was in good spirits. "You know you don't have a thing to worry about. You're part of the family and we look after our own," Deon told Smitty when they first got off the cruise ship. Smitty had a worried look on his face that didn't sit too well with Deon. After all, he was a stranger to the whole crew. He didn't know his role just yet. He was adored for his heart and the fact that he was fearless. He didn't know which position to play. But Deon liked the charismatic young man as he reminded him of a younger version of himself. He knew without direction that Smitty would most likely end up down the same path he did, in jail. He wanted to prevent that from happening. Deon had yet to learn Smitty's story and struggles. He wanted to clear his mind of worries and enjoy himself for a while.

Smitty had lost his mother to heroin when he was just twelve years old. She lay passed out on the floor in the kitchen with a needle stuck in her arm. Her fix was more important than her own son. Smitty had begged her to stop shooting up, but she never listened. All the promises of going to rehab were just to keep young Smitty quiet. Finally, he accepted his fate and knew that his only way out of his situation was to make sure he looked out for his mom. Smitty started slinging at the age of ten. Every night before he went in the house he would make sure that he got enough heroin for his mother. He always made sure it was the good stuff that could get her the hit that she wanted. At that age, he couldn't tell the difference in potency in heroin. Smitty was schooled by an older dealer who used mostly young kids to help move his product around the neighborhood, but Smitty wasn't taught how pure or potent heroin could be. He had been convincing Smitty to sell for him for a while until Smitty struck a deal with him that would supply his mother with an unlimited amount of drug to get high. He only wanted to get her enough drugs to get her high.

Smitty had seen the relief that the drug brought to his mother and he wanted to continue to keep her happy. The wrapping of the leather belt around her arm while searching for a healthy vein to insert the smack into her body had become a routine visual for Smitty. At times when she was struggling, he would assist in pulling the belt around her arm to allow her the freedom of inserting herself properly. Smitty had grown immune to the affects of that image and the obvious pain that his mother suffered from her addiction. The relief that came after each injection was a sight to be seen. Smitty's mom transformed to a completely different person. When she was high, she didn't beat him or yell at him for no reason. She was relaxed and laid back. He enjoyed that side of her and he wanted to make sure he kept her in that state as much as possible.

Smitty was also a tough kid who fought his way through the streets. He rarely lost a fight and those that he did lose; he avenged until his opponent succumbed to him and became fearful of him. The day that Smitty's mom passed was a somber day in his life. His fragile young heart couldn't handle the death of the only parent that he knew. He sobbed most of the day and cried until he had no more tears left. The dealer that he worked for paid for his mother's burial, but Smitty became indebted to him for a long time. At the age of twelve, he had no idea what a funeral cost, so he accepted the twenty-thousand dollar price tag that the man told him he paid for the funeral that was attended by Smitty, the neighborhood drug addicts who knew his mom, and his friends. The man would hold his mother's funeral cost over his head for many years until Smitty had enough and lost it.

Smitty officially became a man at the age of twelve after the death of his mother. While hustling on the street, he continued to pay the rent for the subsidized apartment that the welfare department had given to his mother for a fee of seventy five dollars a month. Though he was raking in close to ten thousand dollars a month for the dealer, he only saw just enough money for him to pay his rent, buy food and clothes every now and then. This went on for two years until Smitty started doing the math monthly. The monthly revenue he was bringing in had also increased over the two-year period, but his salary didn't. When he talked to his boss about an increase in pay, the dealer had the nerve to tell him, "You little fucking ingrate! I buried your crackhead ass mother for a lot of money. You think that debt is paid yet?" "I do believe that I've paid you more than enough and I'm grateful that you buried my mother. I would appreciate if you'd stop calling my mother a crackhead. She's dead and gone, let her rest in peace," Smitty said calmly to the dealer. "Look, you little bastard, I made you. Without me, you wouldn't have been able to eat or live anywhere. You don't fucking tell me what to say. Your fucking mother was crackhead and her stupid ass is gone because of it," he told Smitty. The man only wished he could've retracted his statement. The furor in Smitty's eyes alone was enough to rip out the dealer's heart. Smitty hadn't yet started packing a gun, but he knew that the dealer was always strapped. When he lunged at the dealer with the hammer that he carried by his side like a gun, the dealer didn't know what hit him. Blood gushed out as the hammer landed right at the dealers left temple and his lifeless body dropped to the floor instantly. Smitty got on top of him and bashed his head until he was out of strength. When he left the dealer's apartment, he took all the money and guns that was in site and never returned to Hartford where he was originally from.

Since Smitty had grown to 6ft tall, 160lbs and a very handsome face highlighted by a medium brown complexion by the age of fourteen, many people thought he was an adult. He used that to his advantage when he arrived in Boston to rent a room in this rooming house on Blue Hill Avenue where the lady was more than happy that the handsome young man offered to pay a full year's rent upfront. Smitty arrived in Boston with a bag full of money, his clothes, two handguns, and killer instincts without a plan. Smitty had been living at the lady's house for a couple of months before she decided to set him up. Since he was able to pay her in full for the place for an entire year, she figured he had more money hidden somewhere in his room. She was able to get two men to break into Smitty's room while he was out and about and the men discovered his money in a couple of shoe boxes hiding in the closet. Smitty knew it was a set up from the very beginning. He pulled out his gun and went straight after the woman. She didn't even know what hit her when Smitty started to pistol whip her. He forced her to call the two bandits back to her house with the money and he shot them both in cold blood in front of her. He also took a knife and drove it through the lady's hand and promised to kill her if she went to the police.

As quiet as it was kept, Smitty's actions was known by everybody no sooner than the day after it happened. Smitty soon developed a reputation as a stone cold killer in Boston and he was feared by many people. One of No Neck's hired soldiers decided to bring Smitty along when they were ordered to take out Mr. Brown's security team. The natural flair, killer instincts and the thirst for blood that Smitty displayed was out of the ordinary and No Neck took notice. It was No Neck who told Crazy D, about the tall skinny boy with the heart of a warrior.

While the other members of the crew were in their rooms smashing some of the most beautiful women that they had ever seen, Smitty was trying to fend off the two young ladies who wanted nothing more than to please him. "Come have some fun with us," one of them said in a sexy French accent to him. "No ma, I'm good. Y'all go on and have some fun with each other. I'mma be here watching BET," he told him. The television might've been turned on to BET, but Smitty's mind was somewhere else. He was thinking about his future. He wanted some action. He didn't want to be some lame duck sitting around all day mooching off Deon. He was waiting to get involved in something, anything.

Jean Paul's Secret

Jean Paul received a call and immediately excused himself so he could talk in private with the caller. "Sak pase? Kombien moune nou ginyin semaine sa'a?" he asked the caller in Haitian Creole to avoid exposing his personal business to his guests. "It's about two hundred people," the other voice answered in English through the receivers. "Damn, sa bon, paske nap fe ou bel kob semaine sa'a," Jean Paul said before hanging up the phone. No one quite understood how Jean Paul raked in hundreds of thousands of dollars every week, except his business partners. The auto parts chains he started in Haiti a year or so ago were just barely bringing in $20,000 US dollars a month, which is considered a lot of money in Haiti. However, the hassle he had to go through with employees trying to steal from him, people complaining about his prices and extending credit to his customers, was not worth the headache. He had ten stores countrywide and was hoping to open another fifteen stores in a couple of years. The only joy he received from having that business was the fact that he was able to provide jobs to a few people in Haiti in dire need of income. He knew he was helping many people feed their families and that made him feel good at night.

Jean Paul also owned a courier ship that traveled back and forth from Haiti to Miami. He registered the ship under the name of a corporation so he could operate in the United States. As a deported felon, Jean Paul couldn't do business in the United States, but his lawyers helped him find a way around it. His wife who lived away from the mansion in a house he kept in Thomassin, Haiti, was the person behind all of his legit business affairs. A woman with a mind for business, she knew that she would be set for life when she met Jean Paul during his visit to Haiti years prior to his deportation. Jean Paul had just started selling drugs and was focused on stacking his paper. A short vacation to Haiti turned to a two-month stay, a drug connection that would net him millions of dollars, and a wife.

Her name was Marie and she had the looks and the body of a goddess. A Zoe Zaldana clone with a body of a video vixen, Marie commanded attention from men whether good or bad. Girlfriend of a former drug dealer in Miami, Marie was caught with her boyfriend during a routine traffic stop while they drove to their West Palm Beach estate. The driver behind the 500 SL Mercedes sitting on twenty-two inch chrome wheels did nothing illegal as he cruised Interstate 95 at fifty-five miles per hour. Marie had her head rested on his lap and her lips wrapped around his dick as the driver jovially drove home, looking forward to getting some pussy once he got home. The blaring of the light and the police siren caught him off-guard as he was trying to figure what he had done wrong. "There was no possible way that the cop saw him getting a blowjob from his girl," he thought. Police harassment was the first thing that came to mind and a ticket for whatever it was would send them on their way. "Sir, can I see your license and registration?" the cop asked as Marie tried her best to straighten herself up. The pre-cum from the driver's dick didn't get a chance to be spat out the window as Marie was trying to conceal her action. A quick swallow and a flirtatious look towards the officer would not help them. The officer ran a check on the driver's license and everything came back clean. However, it was a K-9 officer, and his K-9 partner wouldn't stop barking. The officer grew suspicious and decided that he wanted to search the car. "Sir, do you mind opening the trunk of your car for me so I can search it?" he asked the driver. "I think I'm within my legal rights if I tell you to get a warrant if you want to search my car, officer," answered the driver. A back-up unit was called and the officer was almost certain that there was something hidden in the trunk of the car. Meanwhile, the K-9 continued with his endless barking. Trained as cokeheads, these K-9 dogs won't stop barking until they get their fix.

By the time backup arrived, the driver was contemplating his next move. The officer felt he had enough just-cause to search the car, so he asked the driver to step out of the car and placed him in the back of his patrol car as his back-up looked on. The K-9 was taken on a short walk around the car and the barks increased with each step. Meanwhile, Marie was separated from the driver and placed in the backup patrol car. They had better gotten their story together before the backup officer arrived. After the officer opened the trunk, to his surprise, it was empty. However, the dog continued to bark. The stash was finally found by the dog in a secret compartment located above the two rear tires. A search of the vehicle's secret compartment revealed ten kilos of cocaine with a street value of over two hundred thousand dollars. The car was impounded while Marie and the driver were taken into custody to the local barrack by state troopers. They were now facing multiple charges for drug smuggling, but the driver decided to turn a snitch and told the cops that the drugs belonged to Marie and he was just driving her car at the time.

Marie had been dating the driver for almost two years. Just like a typical drug dealer's girlfriend, everything he owned was in her name, including the Mercedes that he was driving, due to her great job as a nurse and her perfect credit. She was aware of his drug deals, but had no idea he had drugs in the car on that day. Otherwise, she would not have ridden in the car. That was her rule. Marie had grown accustom to the posh lifestyle that she had been provided with since she met her boyfriend and made no qualm about him being a drug dealer. Now caught in the middle of a twenty-year sentence, she vowed revenge. Marie was left to take the fall for the drugs as the driver walked away scott free. The feds repossessed everything that was in her name and Marie was sent to prison to start her sentence. Her lawyer fought hard to get a reduced sentence to five years, but she was deported after serving four years of her sentence.

Jean Paul met Marie by chance. He and his boy went to Cabane Choucoune, a place where some of Haiti's hottest bands played. On that particular night, Djakout Mizik, one of Haiti's hottest band at the time, was playing. Unlike the States, the women in Haiti would never venture to a club or concert on their own. It has something to do with the culture, but also a lot more to do with lack of finances. Most of the women in Haiti barely have any money to buy food, much less pay for entertainment. They rely on men to take them out and show them a good time. That evening, every woman in the place was accompanied, a situation that Jean Paul wasn't used to. In the States, women are more independent and can always afford to pay their own way into a club. Therefore, they usually outnumber the men. Not only that, but with the famous "ladies night" gimmick going on at clubs all over the country, a man usually doesn't have to worry about finding women in a club in America. It's not like that in Haiti. It was like bumping his head against a cement wall as Jean Paul and his boy continued to look around all night for a single woman. Then out of the blue walked in these two women wearing the tightest dresses and had bodies that were perfect in God's creation. Ass was booming and titties were just popping. Jean Paul and his boy weren't going to let that opportunity pass them by. They shifted to player mode and before the ladies knew it, a waiter was at their table taking their order of drinks, courtesy of Jean Paul and his boy. Bottles of champagne were ordered and Jean Paul happily picked up the tab.

Marie knew from the very start that Jean Paul was not a townie. His swagger and gear had the States written all over it, which was what she was looking for. She didn't want to mess with the men in Haiti because most of them were either too broke for her taste or they lack the style she sought in a man.   Jean Paul and his boy came over and introduced themselves, and they ended up dancing the night away with the ladies. As a matter of fact, Jean Paul spent the whole damn week of his vacation with Marie. At the end of Jean Paul's vacation, all he got from Marie was a kiss, while his boy almost wore out the other girl's pussy that week. Jean Paul wasn't mad because he was already used to pussy. He wasn't fazed. In fact, he was more intrigue than anything. He wanted to see more of Marie. A relationship was established and the two kept in touch over the next year before Jean Paul went down to Haiti and married Marie.

At first, he was embarrassed to reveal his secret to her, but as time went on, he grew comfortable enough with her to let her know that he was a drug dealer, not by choice but out of necessity, according to him. Meanwhile, he kept the money pouring in every month and he spent at least one weekend a month in Haiti with his wife. He was sending thousands of dollars to Haiti every month to build a nice comfortable home for his wife.   Jean Paul may have been honest, but Marie never once revealed her past to him. She was the best actress as she acted like she had never been to the States. She told him she had visited other countries, but never America. She did not look or act like the local women and he knew that. He could tell from the time he met her. She also told him that her entire family perished when hurricane David hit Haiti, which was not the case. There was no way for him to find out any information about her. She worked as a nurse at the local hospital and that was impressive enough to him. He never bothered to ask her where she went to school, because he was mesmerized by her beauty and her persona. Jean Paul was even happy that she hadn't been to America because he didn't want her to become liberated and corrupted like he thought of most American women with their fight for equality. He didn't even question the fact that her English was flawless. She vaguely mentioned she attended the Union School in Haiti, where all courses are taught in English.

Jean Paul was only married to Marie for a couple of years before he was hauled off to prison. He had sent most of his money to Haiti because his plan was to go back and live a quiet family life with his wife. While he was in prison, Marie continued to write him and kept his spirit up. She told him she would be there waiting for him when he got out of prison. He had sent enough money back to Haiti to set them up for life. Marie had even quit her job and started traveling to other countries at her own leisure. He cautioned her not send any money to the States for him because he didn't want the Feds to find out about his stash in Haiti.

Marie's family had turned their backs on her because she had brought shame to them. Her mother and father never once went to see her while she was in prison. And when she was deported, they washed their hands off with her completely. However, Marie was able to use her beauty to get very far in Haiti. Armed only with her college degree, Marie was released to no one's custody when she first arrived in Haiti. One of the top officials at the prison where she was being held in Haiti wanted nothing more than to make her his concubine. And she played the role until he got her out of prison. She also used him to get a job as a nurse with her degree from the University of Miami. In Haiti, it's more about who you know and the official was connected enough to get her a job without anyone questioning her background. She was able to work under the name Sandra Pierre because she had earned her degree under that name. He also helped her obtain a new identity by getting her a birth certificate with the name "Marie Jacques," in case she ever ran into any trouble or wanted to travel out of the country. Her real name was Sandra Pierre, the name she was born with and deported to Haiti by The United States. She was able to forge a new name and identity and she's been known as Marie Jacques ever since. Shortly thereafter, she stopped seeing the high ranking official when she met Jean Paul. She never mentioned her real name to Jean Paul.

After Jean Paul was released to Haitian custody, Marie had to call on her old friend to help get Jean Paul out of prison in Haiti. She told him Jean Paul was her cousin. With the promise of a night of passion, the high ranking official was more than willing to help. After sleeping with the man once more to secure Jean Paul's freedom, Marie had had enough. She threatened to go to the man's wife if he didn't stop harassing her for sex. The relationship was over and she severed all ties with the man. Meanwhile, Jean Paul never could question the tactics his wife used to get him out. He thought she paid somebody off.

Marie had saved most of the money that Jean Paul had sent to her over the years before he went to prison. He had a little over ten million dollars and he wanted nothing more than to invest some of it in a vessel. He was able to use Marie's name to establish a corporation and he bought an iron vessel, used as a former cruise ship, from this retiring man for almost five million dollars. Jean Paul had bigger dreams for the big vessel, which was used to transport goods between the United States and Haiti. Jean

Paul hired a captain and he operated the vessel for the better part of six months as a cargo ship between Haiti and Miami. As time went on, he saw more opportune ways to use the vessel.

With so many Haitians willing to spend their life savings to find a way to get to America, Jean Paul couldn't resist the money. These people would scrape up thousands of dollars just to get on a little raft that could hardly make it to Cuba in the shark infested waters of the Caribbean. But life in Haiti was so hard it was a risk that most were willing to take. Jean Paul's big ship would provide safety from the troubled waters and these people would be guaranteed arrival to their destination in Miami. The smuggling started out Asian style. Jean Paul would load a couple of people in boxes labeled with goods, such as mangos and have his captain deliver the wooden boxes to Miami. A family member would then pick up these people from an agreed warehouse location. Business was decent at $15,000.00 per person and ten people per week. Jean Paul was netting almost one hundred grand a week after paying off custom officers, lookouts and other business associates involved in his dealings. Business started to grow as the demand to flee Haiti increased. One hundred people were being smuggled every week and Jean Paul's business grew to a seven figure weekly business. He never kept his illegal activities from his wife. He had grown to trust her because she stood by him through his bid. However, because of what happened to her in Miami, she requested that Jean Paul have a separate home in case the feds or Haitian police ever come knocking. The residence in Jacmel was Jean Paul's home away from home. His wife lived in Thomassin, which is located about forty-five minutes to an hour from the capital.

Marie was also growing tired of the illegal lifestyle that Jean Paul was not willing to give up. She felt they had enough money to live comfortably until the end of time, but Jean Paul was greedy. Not only that, he also wanted to maintain his lifestyle away from his wife with the other women. His wife had never been to his second home away from home. It was his place of business and he rested his head there four times a week. Marie had gone through many lonely nights while her husband was up in Jacmel having his fun. She never even knew where the other house was located because he never showed it to her. Instead, he had her believe that a three-bedroom condo located in the center of the city of Jacmel was where he laid his head at night when he wasn't home with her. She had been to the condo and she trusted that he was there whenever he said he was.

He thought his game was so tight that she believed everything out of his mouth.

Jean Paul's personal business was kept a secret from Deon because he didn't want to take the risk of someone snitching on him. He was not tied to the ship in any way or form on paper, but he had everything to do with its operation. Jean Paul figured the less Deon knew about his personal life, the better. He also didn't want Deon to become a casualty in case he ever had to go down. Jean Paul only indicated to Deon that he knew the captain of the ship and that was the extent of his relationship to the vessel. Jean Paul was making roughly two million dollars a week of steady income from the operation of his ship. He was living like a king. The chump change he was making from his auto parts stores mostly went to his philanthropic deeds in Haiti. Many kids around the town where he lived were able to attend school daily because of him. He had a well dug in the town where he provided water for the people and he had also established a farmer's market where vendors came to sell their fresh fruits, vegetables and livestock for a minimal fee. He was looked upon as a philanthropic god in the community.

Jean Paul also benefited from the legal cargo that was being transported from Miami to Haiti. That part of the business netted him an additional five hundred thousand dollars of legit money every month. His lifestyle could never be questioned because he was a legitimate businessman in everyone's eyes; at least that's what he thought. No one knew of Jean Paul's wife except those who were close to him. Jean Paul also had a secret entrance to his house that he only knew about. His henchmen never knew when he left his house. "Once I close these doors to my bedroom, I don't want anybody to bother me under any circumstances. If anything has to be handled, you better handle it and tell me about it the morning," he would tell the man who was in charge of his security. When Jean Paul had his house built, he had an underground tunnel built that led to a garage under his house. At night, he would drive to Thomassin to go see his wife without saying anything to his staff. He kept a late model bulletproof, window tinted, Nissan Pathfinder as his personal car. He had two hand guns in the glove compartment. He drove a pathfinder because he didn't want to draw attention to himself.

Marie Jacques AKA Sandra Pierre

Meanwhile, Jean Paul's wife was no saint either. Jean Paul may have been the man who took care of Marie, but she was never in love with him. She loved him for sure, but being in love was not what she sought at the time. She was definitely intrigued with his swagger when they first met, but he was not her type. Like most men with money, Jean Paul thought his money was enough to keep his wife satisfied. His short strokes were fast becoming a problem for Marie. A sexually liberated woman, Marie sought sexual gratification elsewhere when she couldn't get it from Jean Paul. She remembered the first night she decided to give this dude some pussy and his dick was spewing cum within thirty seconds after being inside of her. It was total waste of time and she knew from then on that she would never be satisfied with a man like that. Though more effort was put in his second round, but five minutes still didn't meet Marie's expectation.

Jean Paul just wasn't blessed with any bedroom skills. He was more of a selfish lover than anything. Marie would often be left with a throbbing feeling between her legs needing to reach the heights of sexual gratification on her own. The secret stash of pleasurable, sexual toys that Marie kept under her bed in a shoebox had been exhausted since she met Jean Paul. She wanted an orgasm propelled by some good winding, deep stroking and great cunnilingus. Unfortunately, Jean Paul didn't make up for the lack of his dick use with his tongue. There was absolutely no substitute and the flame between Marie's legs had to be tamed. Jean Paul was the best provider that she could've found in Haiti, but his lack of sexual prowess and overall inability to use the tool that God bestowed upon him forced Marie into the arms of another skinny man by the name of Reginald who used to fuck Marie for hours and made sure she came three or four times every time they had sex. It's been said that many women would choose sexual gratification over money, and Marie would prove that saying true. Having the best that life had to offer wasn't enough to bring contentment to Marie. She had needs and those needs superseded any material possession that Jean Paul could provide for her.

Reginald was not the typical man that Marie would date, but he had a little style. His working family didn't have much, but they made sure Reginald finished school and learned a trade. An autobody specialist by trade,

Reginald owned a small Autobody shop located on Rue Champ De Mars, in the capital city of Port Au Prince. At twenty-seven years old, he stood at an even 6ft tall and weighed about 155 lbs. A little slim for his height, but cut all around. His bow legged suggested that he was packing heavy when she laid eyes on him the first time. She had gotten into a car accident in front of his shop and he offered to fix her car for her for a minimal fee. Blessed with a great smile, strong features, dark piercing eyes and beautiful chocolate skin, Marie was able to look beyond Reginald's dirty denim overall to find a sexy, attractive hard working man underneath.

His smile captivated her right away. She was smitten by the young man who came to her rescue. The thought of this man pounding her pussy to ecstasy was at the forefront of her mind. She imagined him holding her up against the wall with her legs wrapped around his body as he penetrated her pussy so deep that her body would go into convulsions. His presence took away her anger about the accident, momentarily.

Marie left the house that morning wearing a flowing white linen dress, white sandals and a pair of Chanel glasses with a simple brown colored lipstick on her lips. She couldn't hide her natural beauty even if she tried. Her brand new Mercedes Benz, ML 350 was pretty banged up and the driver, who hit her with an outdated hooptie that belonged in the junkyard, had no insurance. She was mad as hell until Reginald appeared in sight. He was trying his best to calm her down, but she wanted a piece of the other driver. A feisty and sexy woman, she started to charge toward the other driver until Reginald stepped in to restrain her. Reginald offered to drop his prices to about twenty five percent in order to help Marie gain her composure. He looked over her car and decided on a price that was more than reasonable in order to gain her business right away. It was more of a personal interest and she recognized it right away. Marie understood the extent of the damage to her car and was amused by Reginald's generosity when he told her the cost to repair the car. Reginald told her that he would make her car a priority and he would have it back to her in two days as long as he could get the parts. Marie agreed to leave her car at the shop while she hailed a taxicab home. She also told Reginald that her name was Marie Sandra Jacques, but everybody called her Sandra. Not that it was necessary because Reginald never called by her name since he met her. "Cherie," translated into darling in English, was the only name he ever called her by.

Reginald and Marie

Reginald was the perfect gentleman when Marie came back to pick up her car a couple of days later. She was surprised that he fixed her car so well and for so little money. The truth is, Reginald's shop had been struggling and business was slow. Marie was so accustomed to US prices; she thought she was getting a great deal. She was overly grateful, and he recognized quickly from her generosity after she gave him an extra hundred dollars as a tip that she was from the States. Marie's accent in her native tongue also made it obvious that she was raised overseas. She was just what Reginald was looking for, a woman who was financially well-off and with the looks and body that any man would desire.

Reginald was a little less aggressive than Marie was used to, but that made him the more appealing to her. He didn't even try to hit on her as she hopped in her car to drive away. She was gone for no more than five minutes when she realized the Mercedes Benz emblem on the hood of her car was missing. She drove back to the shop to address it with Reginald, but before she could get out of her car to say anything, he was standing outside with the emblem in his hand waiting to put it back on the hood for her. It almost seemed as if he had done that before and was rehearsed. "I am sorry, I forget this," he said in English pointing to the emblem as he attempted to impress Marie, as very few Haitians in Haiti speak English. "Oh, you speak English?" she asked curiously. "A litol," he answered. With so many people standing around watching them, Reginald was trying his best to keep them out of his conversation. Haitians have a bad habit of staring and eavesdropping in other people's conversation, a form of rudeness deeply rooted in their lack of formal education. Haiti's illiteracy rate is the highest in the western hemisphere. Public education is almost nonexistent as people still have to pay a nominal tuition fee in order to attend public schools. However, the lack of education has more to do with the chokehold America and the other superpower nations have put on Haiti than the actual people of Haiti, Deon would later learn.

Impressed with his effort, Marie wanted to know how much more well-versed this man was. "So where did you learn English?" she asked. "I took class in school," he said in an improper way. "Not bad," she said. "You go out with me for dinner please?" he asked sounding awkward to her, but his begging face appealed to her. The meeting with

Reginald was almost timely for Marie as Jean Paul had just been picked up by the cops and charged with second degree murder and was looking at a long sentence in prison. She knew it would be a while before she saw him again, and her needs couldn't wait that long even though his sex was unsatisfying to her, she settled. Reginald's bowlegged stance was all that was running through Marie's mind. She just knew that this man was blessed and he would bless her pussy with all that she had been missing. "Sure, I would go to dinner with you," she said hesitantly. "I pick you up at seven o'clock, ok?" he said to her as his exposed pearly whites left a dreamy impression on her. Marie quickly thought about the fact that she was married and told Reginald, "I think it's better if I meet you at the restaurant. As you can see, I'm married and I don't want to get in trouble with my husband," she said while extending her ring finger to him. "I understand. Lucky husband," he told her. "Where do you wanna go?" she asked. "We can go to Harry's and go see a movie after if you want," he told her. "Ok, I will meet you at Harry's at seven o'clock," she confirmed.

While Jean Paul was sending money to Haiti for Marie so she could live a luxurious life, he thought his monthly sexual romps were enough to keep her satisfied until the next time she would see him again. To his credit, she never told him how unsatisfied she was with him sexually in order for him to try to improve. He assumed he was fucking her well enough to make it last each time. After getting locked up, he wrote her a long letter explaining his situation, telling her that he would not be coming to Haiti anytime soon because of his legal battle and incarceration. However, he told her to hold on to the money that he had been sending to her and that one of his boys would continue to send her money while he was locked up. Jean Paul had many people working for him on the streets and his connects were loyal to him because he treated them fairly. Marie was getting even more money every month because Jean Paul was locked up. He no longer had to worry about maintaining his lavish lifestyle on the street, so most of his money went to her for the first year while he was locked up, until his partners got greedy and decided to cut him out completely.

Reginald just happened to be what Marie was looking for as her nights were filled with loneliness and her bed with emptiness while her husband was living in a cramped jail cell in the States. She contemplated the risk involved if she were to get attached to Reginald, but her throbbing pussy was more convincing than her common sense. "I just need an occasional good fuck from this man to keep me sane and I'll be all right," she would say to herself. Marie wasn't sure if she would be able to separate her emotions from the sexual romps she had planned on having with Reginald. She was certain he was gonna get pussy from her, but she didn't know whether or not she would become attached. Marie drove home that day dreaming about a romantic, explosive, sexually fulfilled night with Reginald in the near future.

Though Marie grew up in America, she was still raised with Haitian customs. It's very uncommon for a Haitian woman to have a one-night stand with a man, because Haitian culture usually looks down on these women as loose. Marie thought about that and how Reginald would probably think she was easy if she gave in to her needs. She needed to find a way to suppress her urges.

As planned, she wore a nice fitted pair of Seven jeans, a white short-sleeve button down linen shirt and a white pair of sandals. She was about fifteen minutes late as Reginald stood there anxiously awaiting her arrival. He was holding a rose in his hand when she saw him standing by the pool table watching two men brag about their pool skills. His face lit up when he finally laid eyes on her. As a matter of fact, the whole damn place lit up when she walked in.

The allure of her Bulgari perfume sucked the attention away from the whole damn restaurant. All the men and women were admiring her. She was focused on Reginald as she walked straight up to him and gave him a kiss on both cheeks, which is customary in Haitian culture. "This is for you," he said as he handed her the rose. "Thank you. That's very thoughtful of you," she told him. Reginald's English was not so advanced that he could understand the word thoughtful, so he just shook his head. The guy wasn't proficient enough in English to hold a conversation all night, but he damn sure was going to try.

After the waitress led them to a table, he proceeded to pull her chair for her and then moved across the table to have a seat. "You look buuliful," he said sounding more Haitian than ever. She smiled because she found his accent amusing. "Thank you. You don't look too bad yourself," she responded with a smile. Reginald couldn't even fathom how he landed a date with such a high class and beautiful woman. As much as he would've liked to believe that she could be his, she was already married to another man. The two of them ordered the Haitian delicacy, "Lambi," with rice and beans, fried plantains and salad. They washed their food down with a glass of white wine.

Over dinner, Marie and Reginald had great conversation and enjoyed each other's company. She learned that he was from a family that was once prominent under the leadership of Baby Doc. His dad was a big part of the government during that era and his family prospered as a result. Unfortunately, when Baby Doc's fate took a down turn during a coup in the year 1986, young Reginald and his family were forced into hiding as the Haitian people went after everyone involved in that shady government. His father was eventually found and burned alive in the middle of a street in Port Au Prince. It took his mother years to recover from that traumatic event. Young Reginald was only a few years old. His family moved out of the city to a house that his father had built in Croix Des Bouquets before he died. Reginald learned his father's story from his mother who vowed to never to return to the capital city of Port Au Prince. However, after Reginald graduated from secondary school, he wanted to learn a trade and buy his own shop. He decided to move to Port-au-Prince with the financial assistance of his mother.

It was rumored that Reginald had many siblings fathered by his dad from many different women, but he had only kept in touch with one of them, a brother. Since his dad was married to his mother, after his death, only his mother was left with a comfortable cushion to live on for the rest of her life. Reginald didn't talk much about the brother that he'd known since he was a little boy. He only mentioned that his brother lived in the States and was a few years older than him.

Marie and Reginald ended up at the Capitol movie theatre after dinner. The old Kung Fu film drew very little interest from them even though Jackie Chan took on an army of over 100 men, dropping them one by one with his skilled fists and fancy foot work. Reginald and Marie locked lips in the darkness of the theatre from the time they took their seat in the back corner row. His sensitive touch and soft lips had Marie drenched to the point where she reached out and grabbed a hand full of nine inches of thick meat sitting between Reginald's crotch, filling his pants. There was hardly anybody in the movie theatre at the time and Marie's hunger for love had to be fed.

Reginald was surprised that Marie was so aggressive. He had anticipated maybe a kiss and some necking, but for her to be grabbing on his dick, that was a different kind of pleasantry. He nudged his face down to her breasts so smoothly that she didn't even realize that his tongue was circling around her erected nipples forcing light moans to emerge from under her breath. Reginald was more than an expert as he sucked on each nipple while descending his right hand toward her navel to unfasten her pants. Marie just sat back, enjoying something that she felt had been lacking for a long time in her life, sensuality. Jean Paul had been more than a little rough and selfish with her in the past. Reginald was the complete opposite.

As it started to get more than a little warn inside the theatre, Reginald found himself kneeling between Marie's legs with her pants halfway down her knees while his tongue explored her wet zone. It was as if Leonardo Davinci himself pulled out his favorite paint brush to begin work on his most famous painting, Mona Lisa, as Reginald's tongue curled in and out of Marie's pussy. He took her juices in as she cocked her head back to enjoy the magical brushing of his tongue up and down her clit. "Yes baby," she whispered as she held on to his head. Trying his best to give her full satisfaction, Reginald inserted his middle finger inside her pussy while his tongue continued an indefinite encounter with her clit. "Oh shit, baby, you're gonna make me cum," she told him. At that point, she didn't even care about the two people sitting down in the front row who kept looking back to try to see what was going on. All they knew was that the guy sitting next to her had disappeared and she was whispering for mercy. Reginald had disappeared out of sight down between Marie's thighs and he didn't want to come back up.

By now, he had two fingers inside her overly drenched pussy, trying to find her g-spot, like a treasure hunter looking for gold. And gold he would find within minutes, as Marie held on to the uncomfortable chair to shake one of the best orgasms she has had in years out of her body over Reginald's fingers. Reginald had cemented his place between her legs for as long as he acted right after that little episode in the theatre. Marie could only imagine what kind of pleasurable damage Reginald could do to her with his 9-inch dick. His bowlegged ass was sexier than ever to her and she couldn't wait to see more of him. Marie left the theatre with a Cool Aid smile across her face. That was just the beginning for Marie.

The Unexpected

Everyone had a great time with the women for the next few weeks, but hustlers can't just sit around without doing anything no matter how rich they are. Deon and his crew didn't have to worry about money for the rest of their lives if they wanted to remain in Haiti. However, they were restless as they were not used to any type of relaxation. The abundance of pussy was getting played and Deon wondered what kind of legit business he could get into in Haiti. While going straight was the first option, Deon, however, wouldn't pass up an opportunity to make ten times the amount of money he had if it presented itself. Jean Paul was the only person making moves as his business in Haiti needed his full attention. He never took the time to tell Deon about the illegal aspect of his business with the cruise ship. Since the crew was always bored in the house, Jean Paul decided to take them down to the city with him so they could check out some of his auto parts stores. They went from one store to another while Jean Paul navigated through the horrendous traffic in Port Au Prince.

At Dawn, before heading back to Jacmel, Jean Paul decided to stop by his wife's house to see her for a few minutes while the crew waited in the car. Deon was sitting in the front passenger seat while the rest of the crew was sitting in the back of the eight-passenger Toyota Sequoia truck. Everybody was laughing and joking while the car was running and the air conditioning keeping everyone cool. However, when Jean Paul exited the car, no one bothered to lock the doors. The crew only let their guards down for a second, and it was a second too long. All of the doors in the truck flung open a few minutes later, and before the crew could react, they had guns pointed in their faces. Someone immediately threw what look like an empty brown rice bag over Deon's head and dragged him out of the car while the crew looked on with guns pointed at them. It was too late to react as the kidnappers pushed Deon into a waiting SUV while holding guard the rest of the crew at gun point. The whole crew was ordered out of the Sequoia and the gun men carjacked the Sequoia as they followed the lead car to their destination. The crew watched their leader being driven away in anguish as they felt helpless.

The first thing that ran through Deon's mind as he fought to breathe with the bag over his head was that he had been set up by Jean Paul. He wasn't the only one thinking that way. Crusher ran to the house and banged on the door interrupting Jean Paul's usual quickie that he was trying to get off on his wife. Jean Paul came running out, fastening his belt wondering what was wrong. When Jean Paul was at Crusher's reached, he grabbed him by the neck with a deadly look on his face and said,"You set us up motherfucka! I'm gonna kill you." Jean Paul was not one to walk around Haiti without a gun. Before Crusher could choke the life out of him, he had pulled his gun and held it against Crusher's temple before the rest of the crew could rush him. "Ok, take it easy. I know what this looks like, but I'm an honorable man, I would never do no stupid shit like this to my friends. I Gave Deon my word before he came to Haiti and I intend to keep my word that I would watch out for him," he told the crew while still holding the gun to Crusher's head to keep them at bay.

As panic started to set in, young Smitty thought about being a hero. "Fuck that! Let's rush this mothafucka and teach him a lesson," he said as he attempted to charge towards Jean Paul. "I don't think you wanna do that, young buck," Jean Paul said as he let out a shot close enough to Smitty's face that the vibrating impact of the bullet forced him to retrieve and rethink his position. "This is not a motherfucking negotiation. Deon is my man and I'm gonna make sure we get him back in one piece, but you motherfuckers gonna have to start trusting me. Besides, if I really wanted to set up Deon, wouldn't all you motherfuckers be dead by now?" Jean Paul said to the crew. The crew stood back to let his statement marinate for a few seconds, but still not completely convinced yet. "Even if y'all were do take me out, how the fuck you're gonna find D? You don't even speak the fucking language here," he confirmed. That point hit home with all of them. "Y'all step the fuck back and let my man take the lead on this," Crusher told the crew.

Big Business In Haiti

This was definitely not the kind of action that the crew was looking for, but nevertheless, they will have to act in order to find their leader. Jean Paul quickly ran back to the house to retrieve the key to his wife's Mercedes. The crew hopped in and they started driving back to Jacmel. The first mistake that Jean Paul made was that he left his armed security men back at the house because Cindy didn't feel like going for the ride with them. Not only that, Deon was the first to tell him, "Bruh, we can handle ourselves, you don't need to bring security with us. We're grown ass men. Ain't shit down here we couldn't handle." Deon wanted to show Jean Paul that he was still the tough guy from the States who had saved Jean Paul's ass in prison. Jean Paul didn't want to offend anybody, especially his new friend Deon. However, he always knew the existing threat in Haiti with all the kidnappers running around looking for a payday. Deon also didn't understand that most of the kidnappers in Haiti are stone cold killers who would do anything in order to feed themselves and their family.

Unfortunately, he would find out the hard way how cold these kidnappers could really be.

Nobody's mind was at ease during the ride back. Jean Paul was trying his hardest to figure out which crew might've kidnapped Deon. There were many different crews in Haiti trying to kidnap the Diasporas who returned home for a visit as well as the rich businessmen and merchants who would come to the city everyday to conduct their daily business. Kidnapping was rampant and everybody in Haiti knew to stay alert and keep an eye out for the kidnappers while in the city. Even the businessmen were forced to hire private security when they came to the city to conduct business. Jean Paul knew this and this was the reason why he always had his security team follow him to the city.

Haiti was once considered a haven for anybody with a good business plan to prosper. American companies took advantage of slave-like labor by bringing their factories to the country and set up shop only to pay the workers 10-20 cents an hour to work. Companies like Disney took advantage of the situation without looking at the overall affect of their actions. The Diaspora could no longer go back to their homeland without having to worry about their safety. News reports of the kidnapped being murdered by their captors were rampant. Those victims who were killed were often killed because they couldn't come up with the demanded ransom. And even when a ransom was negotiated, the victims still ended up dead because the kidnappers feared that they would identify them to the police. Jean Paul picked the wrong time to try to educate The Hoodfellas about Haiti's kidnapping history. They had their leader.

Everyone was on edge in the car. Not only was Deon kidnapped, but he was kidnapped in a bullet proof truck that provided protection for the enemy. "How come these guys were able to get to y'all in the car? Did you guys leave the doors unlocked?" Jean Paul asked while driving. The whole crew looked at each other without knowing that they were responsible to lock the door when Jean Paul ran into the house. "Every car that I own in Haiti is bullet proof and I have weapons hidden in every compartment imaginable, just in case some shit like that went down. Why didn't you guys pull out the guns?" he asked agitated. "We let our guards down for just a minute and they took advantage of that opportunity," Crusher told him. "Y'all were too busy talking about all the pussy you got the other night, that's why we got caught off guard. Fuck a broad! I don't give a fuck about no pussy. I ain't getting caught with my pants down in this motherfucka ever again," Smitty said angrily to the crew.

The whole crew looked back at this bold young kid talking as if he was an experienced gangster. They just shook their heads.

"When we get to the house, I gotta make some phone calls to find out which crew kidnapped Deon," Jean Paul told the crew, but before he could finish his statement, his phone rang. "Hello, who's this?" Jean Paul asked on the phone. "I have someone who wants to say hi," a voice said on the other line. Jean Paul signaled for everyone in the car to be quiet while he put the phone on speaker to listen. "JP, it's D. Yo, fuck these muthafuckas, you know I ain't going out like no sucka. Don't give 'em shit!" he said before the phone was pulled away from him and the voice returned. "Here's the deal, Dawg: you're gonna bring us 100 million dollars in two days or you're gonna find this Yankee boy dead on the streets of Port Au Prince with his dick in his mouth. We don't wanna have to hurt him, but he think he's some hard shit. We just might have to teach his ass a lesson. You got 48 hours. We'll call you with a drop-off destination. Don't try to fuck with the Haitian Posse, muthafucka or your boy will get it." All the crew heard was the click of the phone after the man made his demand.

The crew had never been in this position before, so they didn't know what to do or say. Being in a foreign land with a problem of this magnitude with only one friend that they could trust was nerve racking. "What are we gonna do?" asked Crusher while pounding his right fist in his left hand in anger. "Getting angry ain't gonna get shit accomplished. We need to think rationally and come up with a plan to rescue D," Jean Paul told the crew. By now everyone had started to refer to Jean Paul as JP because Deon had given him the nickname the minute he started to refer to Deon endearingly as D. "Yo JP, we gotta find these muthafuckas and kill every single one of them, B. They don't know who they're fucking with," Crusher said to Jean Paul. "You're right, they don't know who they're fucking with, but we also don't know who we're fucking with. These guys can be just as brutal or hard as we think we are. That's why we gotta think rationally to figure out their motive and how they operate," he said trying to appeal to the crew's common sense. "Fuck that, I say we pay somebody to trace the call and we go find these muthafuckas and bury them alive," Smitty said angrily. "Young buck, you got the fire and determination, but you don't have the mental stability yet to deal with a situation like this. It all comes with time and maturity and I can see the fire in you. You will get there some day, but I need you to stay with me on this. I got this," Jean Paul told him.

Smitty immediately started to lash out at Jean Paul. "Man, you ain't got shit. We're driving back to the crib while they got my man holed up somewhere talking about we need a 100 mil to get him out. I'll show these muthafuckas 100 mil," Smitty said, still angry. Jean Paul tried his hardest to stay calm while he listened to everyone's concerns. "Look fellas, we can try to take care of this logically so we can get D back in one piece and kill those bastards who kidnapped him, or we can go on emotions and end up getting D killed while our black asses also get killed in the process. We don't even have enough guns in this car to go to war with these muthafuckas. I also need to tell you a little bit about the history of this group before we move forward, so that you know how to deal with the enemy," he told the crew.

The Haitian Posse

Everyone was intently listening in the car as Jean Paul went into the history of the Haitian Posse. "One of the worst kidnapping crews in Haiti is the 'Haitian Posse,' a crew consisted of deportees from the United States who had committed heinous crimes before being deported back to Haiti. Most of them had served at least 5 to 10 years in a US prison before being sent back to their homeland like myself. They are definitely proficient in English and their crime syndicate is better than most Haitian syndicates. Most of the deportees involved in the crime of kidnapping get involved once they get to Haiti out of necessity and survival. Often times, these men are returned back to a home and a culture that they know very little about, but because of their resident alien status in the States, they are forced back to their homeland. Half these men don't have a clue about Haitian culture because they spent most of their lives living in the States. They are more American than they are Haitian and everything that they do is done the American way with a little more Haitian desperation added to it." The whole crew listened as Jean Paul spoke and tried to put together the pieces of the puzzle they had to work with.

For one thing, they understood that the members of the Haitian Posse had nothing to lose, but everything to gain as the captors of Deon. Moving forward, they had to figure out the best way to outsmart and outmaneuver the Haitian Posse. Jean Paul wasn't done with his history on the Haitian Posse. He continued, "Most of the time when these prisoners are deported, they're released to the custody of the police in Haiti and are often kept in a jail cell for a period of time, depending on their family connection or how much money they can pay an official to get them out of jail. The jails in Haiti are ten times worse than the ones in the States. Overcrowding and lack of food are just a few of the issues that inmates have to deal with once they get here. Stabbings, rapes and other malfeasances are just part of the order in the prisons in Haiti. An inmate is lucky if he gets one meal a day, and that one meal is usually consist of corn meal and a glass of water, something a pig wouldn't even eat. These muthfuckas are hard up down here and they'll do anything to survive." All the crew could say was "Dammmmmn!" They thought they had it bad in prison in the States, but they didn't have it half as bad as those jailed in Haiti.

Jean Paul didn't sugarcoat anything, including his own situation. He told the crew how he was afraid that he didn't think he was going to make it out alive while he was in prison in Haiti when he was first deported. They all knew that Jean Paul was not soft, and for him to have been scared like that, shit must've really been bad. "JP, what do these people do after they get outta prison down here?" Tweak asked. "Man, ain't shit to do. That's why they form these gangs and they start kidnapping muthafuckas for ransom. First of all, ain't no job in this fucking country; second, they look at prisoners as the scum of the earth and third, the government ain't doing shit but filling up their pocket with the country's money. Muthafuckas gotta eat, so they do what they have to do. Some of them kidnappers are cops too. Most of these gang members can only get their guns from the Police Department. It ain't like the States where you can find guns for sale on every corner," Jean Paul told them.

"Yo, are we really gonna give these muthafuckas a hundred million dollars?" asked Smitty, still agitated with the situation. "Nah, to be honest, I don't want to give them shit. However, the way this business works down here, they always come up with a high number in hopes of negotiating to a realistic amount. Most people in Haiti end up negotiating with them without getting the police involved. And too many people in Haiti believe that the police are already involved to begin with, so they usually pay the ransom to save their family members. There's a lot of dirty cops down here. I have quite a few of them on my payroll," Jean Paul revealed. By the time Jean Paul was trying to finish making his point, the crew had reached their destination in Jacmel to Jean Paul's house. The big steel gate was opened by the gerand after hearing the sound of the horn beeped. Jean Paul drove the car into the yard and everyone jumped out.

Emotional

Cindy couldn't contain herself after hearing that Deon had been kidnapped. Though she had been around the other members of the crew for a while now, she only felt comfortable with them when Deon was around. As a white girl, she never felt that sense of belonging without the presence of Deon. "Oh my fucking god! What the hell happened?!" she screamed hysterically. "We're gonna get him back. Calm down. We just have to come up with a plan. I'm sure JP has a plan already," Crusher assured her. "We gotta get him back! We gotta get him back!" she kept screaming at the top of her lungs. Cindy was visibly shaken at the thought of possibly losing Deon to the kidnappers. "What am I gonna do without him?" she said out loud hoping to receive some comforting words that all was not lost. "Cindy, don't worry yourself too much about this. I just have to make some phone calls to get to the bottom of it, but more importantly I need to find out how the kidnappers knew our whereabouts," Jean Paul told her.

Just as Cindy was getting emotional, Maribel joined in with her own emotion. She didn't fully grasp what was going on at first, but when she noticed that Deon wasn't with the crew, she looked to Jean Paul and said, "What happened, papi? Where's Deon?" Jean Paul really didn't feel like dealing with two emotional broads, he walked towards his office leaving Crusher to deal with the two women.

Over the past few weeks Maribel, Cindy and Deon had created a special bond and they were starting to really like each other. Maribel was the person who kept Cindy occupied whenever Deon was with the boys. She and Cindy were becoming good friends as well as lovers who admired the same man. Cindy understood that Maribel had the aesthetic appeal that Deon sought in a woman, but his heart belonged to her. She also liked being with Maribel sexually and didn't mind sharing her man with her. The goal was always to keep Deon happy and both women had been trying their best to make sure that happened the last few weeks.

Crusher tried his best to assure the two women that their leader would soon return to the house, even if their lives depended on it. Maribel was unlike Cindy, she was ready to go to war with the Haitian Posse. The Hispanic blood running through her veins brought out the warrior in her. "You might want to save your tears for a better occasion, because there won't be any tears shed for Deon. We're gonna find him," Crusher told Cindy confidently before walking out to join the rest of the fellas.

The 411

Jean Paul's position was not made any easier by trying to keep a cool head. This contemptuous feeling among the crew made him edgy and antsy. While he wanted the crew to believe that he had nothing to do with Deon's kidnapping, he knew in a hustler's heart of heart that it looked too suspicious to convince these guys that he wasn't a double-crosser. Jean Paul was racking his brain trying to figure out what went wrong and how someone was able to get to them. He made phone calls after phone calls trying to negotiate the release of Deon without having to go to war with the Haitian Posse, but the Haitian Posse leader refused to accept his bargaining options. Jean Paul knew that the Haitian Posse was all too aware of the fact that he had one of the top security team that Haiti had to offer, but yet, they weren't fazed by his position. However, what they didn't know was that every single female who lived in that household with Jean Paul had been trained in guerilla warfare in the Dominican Republic by an ex-army commander who befriended Jean Paul during one of his trips to that country.

Maribel, Nadege, Rosie, Evelyne had all been trained by the commander. They all knew how to handle many different weapons and had one-on-one combat training. Jean Paul himself was trained by this guy as well as his wife. The women were Jean Paul's secret weapon and nobody knew of their special training background. Maribel almost let out her secret when she started to get emotional over Deon, but she caught herself before anybody suspected anything. If needs be, Jean Paul knew that he could always rely on his women to find out the information he needed about the whereabouts of the Haitian Posse. Jean Paul also had his ears to the streets at all time. His information officers on the street were trying their best to find out where Deon was being held, but everyone was tightlipped on the street about the kidnapping.

There were rumors that the intended kidnapped victim was supposed to be Jean Paul and not Deon, but Deon became a victim of circumstance. There had been many failed kidnapping attempts on Jean Paul in the past, the kidnappers never wanted to give up on trying, even though many of them had been killed by Jean Paul's security team. They were relentless in trying to score a big payday. Word on the Streets in Haiti was that Jean Paul was a billionaire, or one of the richest men living in Haiti, but that was far from the truth. However, Jean Paul never dispelled those rumors either. Instead, he started to encourage that belief in order to keep law enforcement from harassing him and his team. His legitimate businesses made far less money than people knew, but Jean Paul was never one to cry about money. He fed those on the street who needed food, and he was generous to many nonprofit organizations in the country. Those who loved him loved him with all their heart. And those who hated him just wanted all that he had. He knew this.

When Deon and The Hoodfellas decided to come to Haiti, Jean Paul knew that they were gonna be the kings of Haiti. The amount of money that Deon brought with him was enough to help Jean Paul realize his dream of owning, "Ile De La Tortue," an island located off the coast of Haiti that he wished to turn to a resort that would generate billions of dollars annually. Jean Paul hadn't even mentioned his business plan to Deon yet, but he knew that Deon would be down to partner with him in his business endeavors. He saw his dreams going down the tube and also his integrity as a friend and hustler who lived by the code of the streets, being challenged by The Hoodfellas, and he wanted to correct that. His plan was to make everybody rich and they wouldn't have to worry about money for the rest of their lives.

First, Jean Paul needed to find out the necessary information to make sure Deon was not hurt and tried to get the kidnappers to meet him half way with the negotiations. A few more phone calls landed him an important ally who's usually the "go-between" guy for the kidnappers and the kidnapped. Unfortunately, Jean Paul was led to believe that Deon was taken into the slums of Cite Soleil, where the Haitian National Police didn't even bother going into when there was a problem. However, this situation was never about getting the police involved. Jean Paul wanted the information for his own sanity. Though the gang was spread across the city, the harshest part of the group chose the slums of Cite Soleil where they inflicted their pain and almost ninety five percent of the victims never make it out alive, according to hearsay. That information did not rest peacefully on Jean Paul's mind.

Trying to keep a level head while negotiating for Deon's release would be hard for Jean Paul and critical in the next few hours. He didn't want the Hoodfellas to panic and get all riled up without knowing the intricate details and the magnitude of the situation. Jean Paul continued to go back and forth with the guy who was the bridge between him and the Haitian Posse leader. He found out the man's name was Francois. After talking to Francois on the phone a few times, he realized that Francois himself was afraid of the Haitian Posse leader known as "Big Toutou," to everyone in Haiti. Even the cops were afraid of Big Toutou.

Big Toutou

Jean Paul wanted to find a way to talk to Big Toutou himself, but Big Toutou has never talked to a member of anybody's family that he has kidnapped since he got involved in the kidnapping business. He was known as a man who inflicted pain and would go through any length to make sure his demands were met. His bullet riddled body was evidence that he was fearless and heartless when it came to killing without cause. He received his wounds while escaping the grasp of police after a set-up. For a while, everyone in Haiti thought he was dead because there was no way anyone expected him to survive twenty-two gunshot wounds to his body at the hands of the police.

Known as a kid simply as Toutou, he grew up like any child born into poverty in Haiti. He was the youngest of nine children. His mother birthed all those children by four different men. Most of the children were born in set of two's per man, except for one man who stuck around longer than the rest to have a third child with Toutou's mother. Each man walked out on her without ever supporting his kids. Toutou and his sister were the last pair of children his mother had before she allowed one last man to walk out on her. She vowed never to love a man again and to never have children again after Toutou was born. Toutou was still in the womb when his father walked out on his mother. Toutou pretty much grew up a vagabond wondering the streets of Haiti from a very young age. At five years old, he was at the airport begging the visiting tourists for change as they landed in Haiti. His charismatic smile usually won over the white tourists who felt pity for the little boy who seemed to be a grown man in a child's body, the way he fended for himself. Toutou was undeniably tough as he had to fight through crowds of children at the airport in order to get to the tourists to even beg for the change that he received from them. Often times, the bigger boys would try to take his money from him, but he would stand and fight with rocks, sticks or anything he could find to defend himself.

Toutou's begging on the street didn't only benefit him, but also his mother and his brothers and sisters who were home most of the time without anything to eat. The makeshift shack made up of recycled wood found on the streets and a tin roof also collected from the trash in the streets, housed the whole family. It was a one room shack not even big enough to house one person, much less ten people. Toutou was happy that he helped contribute to the little food that was available to eat at the house. By the time he was six years old, three of his siblings had left the shack to go find their own way in the streets of Port Au Prince. Toutou often wondered where his siblings were, but he was too busy worrying about his mother to go and tried to find them.

A few years had passed since Toutou and his family had heard from the siblings who had left home. By then, three more siblings had left, leaving Toutou and his two sisters in the little shack with their mother. Meanwhile, his mother tried as much as she could to hustle whatever she could find on the street. She would sell oranges, bananas, corn, just anything to try to feed her kids. However, more than anything, she wanted a couple of her children to get an education. The only two of her children with a remote chance of having an education were the two younger girls who were still living at home. She could never scrape enough money to pay the tuition at the public "Lycee," (a public primary and secondary school) that the girls attended. Lycee Toussaint is one of the state sponsored schools in the capital of Haiti, but unlike the United States, state sponsored schools in Haiti still require a monthly tuition. Though the cost of tuition is comparably low to the private schools, it is still a struggle for the parents with no money to send their kids to school. Uniforms are required in most schools in Haiti, but for a parent who is poor, that's just one more hurdle that they would have to deal with. Toutou took notice of the situation at home at a very young age, and he knew that there was no way that his mother could afford to send him to school. He chose his fate and the street was where he wanted to make his living, whether as a beggar, hustler or criminal.

By the time Toutou reached age fourteen, he found out that one of his sisters who left home in search of a better life was killed while working as a prostitute on the street. His two oldest siblings also contracted AIDS and died by the time he was fifteen. Watching all this turmoil throughout his life propelled Toutou to do something that he had never thought about doing. He was only seventeen years old when he boarded a small raft with a group of people to head to Miami. He watched most of the people on the raft perish in the shark infested waters to Florida. By the time they reached close enough to Miami in hopes of a better life, the coast guard intercepted them, Toutou and a couple of other survivors who lasted through the whole trip were picked up, jailed and retuned back to Haiti a year and a half later, after many appeals to the court. That experience transformed him and dashed all his hope for a better life in America.

While in prison at Guantanamo Bay, where the US Department of Immigration housed all the illegal immigrants trying to enter the United States, Toutou met quite a few other desperate men who shared his similar experience. They talked about the fact that they had to shine shoes, wash cars in the gutter and even push a two-wheel wagon in order to earn a living in Haiti that barely kept them fed, or even alive in some cases. Those men were fed up and decided that they didn't want to live like animals anymore. While at the prison, they also learned some English and devised plans to change their lives once they were returned back to their homeland.

There were also hardcore criminals from Jamaica and Trinidad at Guantanamo Bay awaiting deportation. Toutou was a very ambitious young man, so he befriended a man from Trinidad who suggested that kidnapping tourists and other rich people in Trinidad was a lucrative business. Toutou listened to the man and took into account all the risks involved with that type of business. It was also the first time in Toutou's life that he had eaten two meals a day. Despite the fact that the food was not gourmet, it was the best food that he had ever had over the last few years of his life. While in prison, he also shot up six inches in height and gained an unbelievable amount of weight during those few months he was incarcerated. He spent his leisure time in the yard working out and started to develop a muscular build.

Toutou had taken it upon himself to get on the raft and tried to leave Haiti without notifying anybody in his family. He knew that his mother would try to talk him out of it and he didn't want to disappoint her. His mother worried for months because she hadn't seen her son. Just like his other siblings, she figured he was dead and she would eventually have to confirm it for sanity sake. It wasn't like she could afford a proper burial for him, anyway. Meanwhile, Toutou was excited about his deportation back to Haiti. He didn't even develop a glimmer of hope when his court appointed attorney kept telling him that he would fight his deportation as hard as he could. Toutou already saw the prejudicial evidence of US immigration laws and policy towards Haitian while he was at Guantanamo Bay. Everyday, he saw the Cubans being given papers and political refugee status to stay in America because of their lighter skin. He also learned from one of his Cuban friends in prison who was an international history professor, the history of Haiti and Haitians in America. The professor went on, "This racist country would never offer the same opportunities to rebellious Negroes who fought for their freedom against the world's most notorious French army under the command of Napoleon and won. Not only that, he also knew that the ungrateful US government would never grant, a group of heroic Negro soldiers who fought alongside of US soldiers against the French to help them secure the Louisiana Purchase from the French as well as the great battle of Savannah, asylum into the country. If any group deserves clemency from the United States government once they reach American soil, it should be the Haitians. The US government owe them that much. However, memories of Nat Turner, Marcus Garvey and other revolutionaries who fought against slavery in America because they were inspired by the Haitian Revolution against the French, continue to linger in the minds of many people in the US government. And it's only right for them to make sure they show the world that black people can never stand up to white folks. Unfortunately, they can't rewrite history. The Haitians stood up and won with heart and strength against an army thought to be the best and greatest at the time. It is because of that Haitian people in Haiti continue to live in such dismal poverty. The US policy towards Haiti has everything to do with the state of that country." Toutou not only was schooled by his Cuban friend who knew more about Haitian history than he did, but he also was taught to appreciate his culture in spite of what is said about them in the media.

When Toutou found out his last appeal had been denied, he wasn't sobbing like the rest of the Haitians who saw no hope in going back home. Toutou never set out to be a criminal, but society forced his hands and he had to do what he needed to do in order to survive. Toutou returned to Haiti equipped with knowledge, a thirst to help the poor, determination, intimidating physical stature and a yearning for an overall better life. He was rejuvenated while in prison. It was also the first time he ever got a chance to learn to read. Some of the guards found his charisma addictive. They also helped teach him how to read and write. A Haitian born man learned how to read and write for the first time in prison at Guantanamo Bay, a place that is so foreign to his homeland that it was incredulous. Toutou could only read and write in English, though, which didn't really serve much of a purpose to him once he arrived in Haiti, a country where the official language is French, and those who didn't speak French were looked down upon because the language was often learned at school.

Toutou returned to Haiti with a new attitude and fervor for life. A couple of the homeboys he met in prison were more than happy to become part of his new plan.

Toutou was a man with a plan, but without any connection to implement his plan. The only ally he was able to find was a former "Tonton Macoute" who had fallen from grace after the departure of former president, Jean Claude Duvalier, from office. The Tonton Macoute himself had fallen on hard time after the community found out that he was part of the Duvalier regime. The man had originally become part of that regime in order to protect and feed his family. Back then, anybody who wasn't part of the Duvalier regime had a hard time feeding their families. Though he never committed atrocious crimes against anyone publicly when the regime was around, a few people remembered him as a member of that regime. His life was spared when the people took to the streets to revolt against that regime back in 1986. The man claimed he only wanted to look out for the people in his community when he became part of the regime. He made sure his neighborhood was safe and nobody was persecuted by other Tonton Macoutes in the regime, the primary reason why he joined in the first place.

His name was Antoine Pierre Louis. He lost everything that his family ever owned because of his association with the Duvalier regime. His only possession when he met Toutou were the guns that he had kept hidden in a box buried in a hole that he had dug up in his backyard prior to the departure of Duvalier. He didn't even know Duvalier flee the country until 48 hours later. Toutou brought hope to the man and lifted his spirits when he told him about his plan. They were sitting on the bench at "Champs De Mars," a park where people in Haiti gather mostly on Sundays. Toutou and Antoine had been meeting at the park on the bench for a few weeks as they were both homeless. It was Antoine who gave Toutou the nickname "Big Toutou," because of his seemingly huge size compared to the rest of the unfed people around the park who hadn't eaten a full meal in Lord knows how long.

Before Big Toutou revealed his plan to Antoine, he made sure he got a good read of his state of mind. Antoine had nothing to lose. He was in his late thirties and had lost everything that he had worked hard for. His wife left him and he was just of reminder of what used to be one of the strongest regimes in Haiti, a has-been. Antoine jumped at the opportunity to join Big Toutou in his quest to have a better life and help those around him. While Toutou was gone from Haiti, his heart never left the slums of Cite Soleil. It was there that he left all his childhood friends who shared his experience who wanted desperately to live a better life. After Antoine showed him the guns and ammunition that he had buried, Toutou became very enthusiastic. Big Toutou went back to the neighborhood that he had been staying away from since his return to Haiti, to recruit some of the hungriest people that the planet has ever seen. Within a month, the Haitian Posse was formed and they were ready to change their status and situation. Every single member of the crew was armed and ready to kill anybody who got in their way. They held fort in the heart of the ghetto where they protected the people as well as themselves from police and other dangers.

Antoine was the general counselor to the group, not only because of his age, but because he knew the rich targets in Haiti because of his past dealings with them while he was part of the government. He used to see who came to the palace to pay off the government for whatever favor they requested and knew how to get to them. Though he wasn't directly involved when those deals went down, but sometimes he had to provide security for some of the rich folks who sought help from the government. It was also those same people who raped the ghetto of all its resources during the Duvalier era. While they lived up in a mansion on the hill at night, during the day their businesses strived in the hood, and most of them didn't even understand the meaning of the words "give back or community."

The Initiation

Big Toutou and Antoine decided the first victim of their crime syndicate would be a relatively known man in Haiti who owned a store downtown where the street merchants and vendors could come and buy everything, including rice, beans, cornmeal, olive oil, spaghetti, and other foods in bulk at wholesale prices, so they could sell them on the street for a profit. One of the reasons the man was targeted was because he kept raising his prices on the vendors and the people vented their displeasure with him publicly and he never tried to change his position. He forced their hands because he was the first to raise his price and asked his cohorts to the same. He used to solicit the assistance of the government in order to enforce his prices. Antoine remembered him clearly because he would always bring bags of rice and beans to the palace as a form of payment for the favors. The big wigs in the government would turn around and give the food to the lower ranking guards as they were only interested in cash. However, all favors had to be enforced.

At the time, the store owner didn't even need to walk around with security. His reputation as a "gro moso" preceded him. He walked around with a loaded .45 around his waist and he could shoot or kill anybody he wanted to without having to face justice. Arrogant was a light term to describe people like him in Haiti. A very light skinned "mullato" of mixed heritage, known to most Haitians as part of the elite in Haiti, he thought he controlled the world with his money. He never saw it coming that day after he closed his shop and paid each of his employees less than two dollars for a hard day's work, after his business raked in more than $20,000.00 daily. Antoine had knowledge of this because those people were never quiet about the amount of wealth they amassed.

With the black bandana covering half their faces and a few happy fingers on the trigger, Big Toutou and his men forced the store owner into his brand new Toyota Land-cruiser at gun point. The man had to time to react as the barrel of the gun hit the side of his face once he was inside the car. Antoine was behind the wheel as they quickly made it back to the slums of Cite Soleil in the brand new car. The money that the store owner carried in his 'Man purse' counted to be about $22,000.00 US dollars when converted. The money belonged to Big Toutou and his crew, and it was time for celebration. The store owner pleaded for his release, but not before he heard Big Toutou's demand of $500,000.00 US dollars to let him go. The man was tied up, blindfolded and taken to an unknown location where three men kept watch on him at all times. He had no idea what was going on because the Haitian police had not yet started to deal with that type of crime.

Meanwhile, Big Toutou decided to feed everybody in the slum who hadn't eaten a good meal in a long time, with the money he took from the guy. Everybody was in a festive mood as they all feasted on "Fritay" all night long. Every "Machann Fritay" within a mile radius of Cite Soleil was sold out of all the "Fritay" they had planned on selling through the night within minutes. In Haiti, "Machann Fritay" are known street vendors who sell fried pork, plantain, fried beef, Haitian chicken fingers or marinade, Acra, a special Haitian fried favorite, fried sausage, fried sweet potato and fried chicken. The actual foods that the vendors sell are called "Fritay." After eating, everybody washed their food down with a "Kola Couronne," a well-known soda beverage in Haiti. Everybody benefited from the first kidnapping; the street vendors sold all of their food, the people in the slum got fed and the children saw a better day without having to go to sleep hungry one more night.

The store owner's family agreed to the ransom and the man was released. While in the custody of the Haitian Posse, the man was never harmed in any way, shape or form. That first hit pretty much set the Haitian Posse in motion for many more kidnappings and with each kidnapping, Big Toutou spent most of the money on improving the lives of the people in the slum. He paid for many children to attend school and fed families daily. While his goal was to provide everyone in the slums of Cite Soleil with a better life, they had also become his protector as well. Nobody, including the police, could force entry into Cite Soleil without an army of people standing to defend it. Many warrants for the arrest of Big Toutou had gone un-enforced because Cite Soleil was like a fort where Big Toutou was treated like a god and everybody was willing to die to protect him. Big Toutou never set out to get rich from the kidnappings; he only wanted to provide hope and dreams to the kids in the ghetto. His philosophy was to rob the rich to give to the poor, but somewhere along the lines, dissention in his camp and the greedy ways of mankind started to force a shift in philosophy within the group. Like the confident leader he was, Big Toutou felt that he could control the situation and trusted that the men he put in charge would make sure his orders were followed.

Marie's Affair

Even after Jean Paul returned back to Haiti, Marie couldn't stop seeing Reginald. The day that Deon was kidnapped, she had plans to go see Reginald. When Jean Paul came to the house unannounced for a quickie, she acted like she was on her way to the store, and pleasantly surprised to see her husband. Part of her was pleasantly surprised because Jean Paul spoiled his wife with material gifts. He brought her a diamond tennis bracelet. At times, Marie fought with the idea of continuing to stay married to Jean Paul, but her loyalty and allegiance to him kept her in the marriage. She loved her husband but she didn't know how to tell him she wasn't happy with their arrangement. Marie wanted a man who was around at night to hold and caress her and make her feel like a woman, but Jean Paul wasn't that man. She felt like they had more of a business arrangement than a marriage. Marie had made it clear to Reginald that she loved her husband and there was no way she was going to leave him for Reginald. Jean Paul also made it hard on his wife to be faithful because he was so far away in Jacmel and she only saw him two-three times a week. Her fire needed to be doused at times and Reginald's snake was the only remedy. She made Reginald aware of the fact that her husband was a very powerful man with a lot of money and they had to be very careful in their dealings.

Marie was looking sexy as usual and Jean Paul couldn't resist the site of her in a denim mini-skirt, high heeled shoes and a halter top looking like she was about to run the town. He had never been suspicious of his wife's cheating. After handing the gift box containing the bracelet to his wife, Jean Paul proceeded to kiss her neck. She acted like she wanted him but her mind was really on Reginald who had promised to tear her pussy to shreds before she quickly hung up the phone on him when Jean Paul walked through the door. Jean Paul turned around and lifted her skirt so he could penetrate her from behind. Since the fellas were waiting in the car outside, he had very little time to please his wife, so a quickie was in order. That had been the case with many of Jean Paul's visits to his wife's house in the past. A quickie was all she ever got from him, and it was never good enough to make it last, the two minutes that he was inside of her. He blamed his lack of dick control on his lack of time. He was always on the go. When he occasionally spent the night with her, he blamed his lack of passion and sexual inability to last more than five minutes, on fatigue.

Marie had been getting served by Reginald for a while and she was addicted to his dick. Reginald tried to get her to invest money in his business but she refused. He wanted so much to enjoy part of the luxurious life she was living, but she had set the parameters on their relationship. She occasionally bought him a few shirts, pants and shoes, and took him out to eat, but that was the extent of the spending on him. She didn't want to take her husband's money to pamper another man. She always made it clear to Reginald that he was not obligated to continue to see her. He served a purpose in her life and that's all she wanted from him. She wasn't trying to get caught up in him, but she always felt like she was on cloud nine after one of their sexual encounters.

The last time she met with Reginald, they were at the El Rancho hotel located in the heart of Petion Ville. The two of them ate dinner, gambled a little and then headed to the room where Reginald proceeded to make her feel like a woman all over again. The nine-inch flashlight down his pants was lighting down her tunnel, even as she leaned over the roulette table to place her last bet before they left the casino. Reginald was as much a breast man as he was an ass man. He pulled Marie towards him against the wall the minute the door shut behind them and proceeded to kiss her sexy lips without giving her time to come up for air. The harmonious wrestling of their tongues while he massaged the back of her head, sent chills running down Marie's body as if it were a forbidden feeling that she was not supposed to experience. "When something feels so good, it's hard to believe it's real," Marie thought as Reginald continued with his tongue treatment down to her breasts. She let out a sigh of relief and let loose her tension as Reginald seductively massaged her breasts with his tongue. Her nipples stood the most erected that they had ever been, as the motion of Reginald's tongue continued to wrestle away any problems that may have been on her mind.

Marie couldn't believe how great this man was making her feel as she looked down to stare at him caressing her breasts like he wanted to make sure she was satisfied. Marie almost chuckled at Reginald's dedication to pleasing her. She only wished her own husband was so generous. All the material gifts he bought her in the world couldn't stand to the way Reginald made her feel when she was with him. "Cherie, you like that?" Reginald asked as he licked his way down to her navel making sure she was with him all the way. "Yes baby. You make me feel so good," she answered.

He ran circles around her belly button with his tongue. Her body started to shiver. He came up and held her tight while he kissed her passionately. She kissed him back with force this time. Reginald had gotten used to Marie and knew exactly the next route he needed to take to make sure her sexual voyage was satisfying.

The luster of her tongue kept Reginald's tongue wrapped in hers for a few more minutes before he started making his way down to her sugar shack to get a taste of some much needed sweets. She stood still as he enticed her with a finger while kissing his way down her body to her sweet vine. Marie's pussy was drenched as Reginald's finger made music with her clit. The sweet moaning sounds exited her mouth effortlessly. "I hope I don't get so hooked on this man that I can't walk away from him," she thought to herself. The harmony was never broken as Reginald replaced the finger with his tongue keeping her in tune with the rhythm he had created. The pounding of her heart could be felt a mile away as she anticipated a string of orgasms when he gently rubbed his tongue upward on her clit. She stood straight and held on to his head as she shook uncontrollably with her eyes closed and leaving the world behind for but a few minutes.

Reginald had just started. He hadn't allowed her to take her favorite ride for the day just yet. His curved nine-inch dick was hard as steel as she reached down to grope him. She wanted to taste him. A mouth full of grade-A beef was just what the doctor ordered. She squatted down and started to bestow the best blowjob upon him. She took the shaft of his dick in her mouth while massaging his balls with her hands. She needed lubricant. She spat in her hand and tried to jerk him off while allowing the tip of his dick to land in her mouth each time her hand slid down his dick. Reginald almost lost control as his knees came close to buckling under him. He walked over to the bed where she followed behind him anticipating being fucked, well and done. He lay on his back so she could mount his dick like a female jockey. Her pussy glided smoothly down his dick as she jockeyed for the best position to cum. Round and round her hips moved on his dick while he played with her clit. It was hard for him to hold back, so he fought a nut anxiously waiting to exit his body. Her fulfillment was more important to him. As he continued to massage her clit, her movement on his dick increased. "Don't move! Right there, right there," she said as the tension started to ease from her body. Her winding and grinding became stronger as she experienced one of the best orgasms from riding him.

Reginald also took the opportunity to get a nut of his own before she collapsed on him, only to wake up thirty minutes later for another round of doggy style sex.

Reginald decided to keep his position with Marie because that was all she offered to him. As much as he tried to control her with the sex that he knew she was addicted to, he also knew that she would never allow herself to become entranced by his dick. He had made plenty of empty threats where she told him to walk on. She never revealed much about her husband to him except for the fact he was wealthy and powerful. She also made sure that Reginald never came to her house. Jean Paul had reiterated to her the importance of keeping people away from her home for safety reasons. She adhered to his advice and made sure that Reginald understood that her home was off limits and nonnegotiable.

The Negotiations

Jean Paul was tired of talking to Francois and demanded to talk to Big Toutou in order for any type of negotiation to continue. The Hoodfellas were demanding answers and Jean Paul had better give them something to chew on. Jean Paul wasn't going to let some imbecile forced his hands into giving up 100 million dollars, but at the same time, he didn't want to underestimate the captors. The back and forth chatter between Francois ended with Jean Paul slamming the phone down on Francois' ear. After that episode, Jean Paul received a phone call from another man who threatened to cut off both of Deon's feet and deliver them to Jean Paul if he didn't meet his demands. Deon was put on the phone for about five seconds to tell Jean Paul of his beaten state. However, he wasn't broken. He still advised Jean Paul not to pay them shit. Deon had a hard time understanding what was going on because the men only spoke in Creole. Every now and then an English word would slip out from one of the men and he knew that one of them had to have been from the States. Whenever he had to say something to the man in charge, he had a hard time expressing himself in Creole. It was also that man who talked to Deon in English trying to fetch information from him.

"I'm not sure if we gonna be able to negotiate for this Yankee boy with Jean Paul. We don't even know who this man is. Maybe a few more punches to his eye will force him to reveal who he is to us," the man said in his native tongue of Creole, ordering more torture of Deon in the process. Deon was beaten to a pulp and had very little life left in him, but he was a fighter. The kidnappers had no idea who Deon was or what he was doing in Haiti. As far as they were concerned, he was worthless, but they had to find a way to get something for him. "I asked you to bring me Jean Paul, instead, you bring some fucking Yankee that I can't get no money for," the man said loudly to the flunkies surrounding him. The order was for Jean Paul to be kidnapped so they could get the asking ransom from his wife. Instead, they got a big old headache with the heart of a bull. Deon was no longer himself as Crazy D was about to take over. The only thing going through his mind was survival and to get away from his captors. He knew if he allowed them to know who he was they would use that against him to corner Jean Paul into negotiating for their asking price. Based on the conversation these men were having, Crazy D knew that Jean Paul didn't set him up. These men were brutal, hard up for cash and willing to do anything to get it.

After getting nowhere with their antics, the man in charge decided to place a call to Jean Paul acting as Big Toutou. "Hello, who's this?" Jean Paul asked the caller on the other line. "Se gwo Toutou, kiyes ou ye?" the man said on the phone in Creole, identifying himself as Big Toutou. It was a well-known fact all over Port Au Prince that Big Toutou was fluent in English. So Jean Paul proceeded to address him in English. "Okay, you know it's hard to come up with that kind of money and there's no way I can get this much money in two days even if I was the president of Haiti," Jean Paul tried to appeal to the man's common sense. "Kisa blan di?" the man said in Creole, obviously confused and didn't understand a lick in English. Jean Paul quickly realized he wasn't talking to the leader of the gang, Big Toutou, but decided to play along anyway. "Se ayisien ou ye, mwen se ayisien tou, nou pa bezwen nan pale anglais," the man suggested that they speak Creole instead of English since they're both Haitian men. Jean Paul agreed only because he was going along with the man's plan so he could get Deon out.

After going back and forth on the phone and hanging up on each other and the man calling back each time, the demanding price went from 100 million dollars to a negotiating price of 100 thousand dollars, a bargain for Jean Paul to get Deon back, but he didn't want to pay the gang anything. He wanted to teach them a lesson. The whole crew was in the room as Jean Paul negotiated with the man over the phone, but none of them understood anything because all of the conversation was in Creole. Jean Paul had to explain to the crew their position and how he had planned to proceed to get Deon back. Deon's safety was first, but the gang would be taught a lesson that they never expected. It had only been eight hours since Deon was kidnapped. The Hoodfellas felt better knowing Deon was still alive, but more importantly, they at least had a contact and a lead to find out where he was.

Time was running out and everyone was tired, Jean Paul suggested everyone get some sleep so their minds and bodies could be fresh the next day. He wanted to devise a plan to make sure the kidnappers delivered Deon safely and every single dime of the money is burned right along with them. The money was to be burned to celebrate Deon's release, and the people involved to be burned for thinking they had enough balls to pull a stunt like this.

The Breafast Meeting

Everyone was anxious. They woke up very early the next day. The maid had prepared a breakfast consisted of natural scrambled eggs taken straight from one of the hen's nest in the backyard, fresh cooked ham, freshly baked bread and Passion fruit juice. Jean Paul didn't want to burden the members of his security team with the rescue efforts to bring Deon back. He opted to solicit the help of the women he had paid so much money to train in the Dominican Republic, in case something like this ever went down. The Hoodfellas were more than happy to lend a hand and break a few necks in the process. A location for the exchange of money for Deon hadn't yet been revealed by the kidnappers, so Jean Paul wanted to get a jumpstart on the plans to beat the kidnappers at their own game.

Rosie, the girl that Crusher thought was innocent and harmless, was a cold blooded killer from Cite Soleil. She used her beauty and booty to get men to do exactly what she wanted them to do and Jean Paul called on her to go to Cite Soleil to find out if Deon was being held there. More importantly Jean Paul wanted to know how deeply involved Big Toutou was in the shenanigans. In any case, if Deon was being held in Cite Soleil, Jean Paul knew that was impenetrable territory. There was no way he could get his team to go into Cite Soleil to rescue Deon without getting every single one of them killed. Cite Soleil was guarded better than the national palace in Haiti. There were armed guards on rooftops, armed lookouts on every corner, trained snipers ready to shoot from open windows and the people of Cite Soleil themselves ready to die for the man named Big Toutou. Fuck Nino Brown, Big Toutou was the true god in Haiti. He came and saved the people and they would risk their lives for him. Going into Cite Soleil was not an option.

If Deon was being held there, all negotiations had to be done away from there to secure the safety of the crew, but first they had to make sure that Cite Soleil was not the camp. Rosie saw no danger in going back to the place she was born and called home. Everyone in Cite Soleil knew she was one of them and she always received nothing but love when she visited there.

Since Rosie started working with Jean Paul, her lifestyle had been upgraded and her taste in clothes had taken a dramatic shift for the better, but she couldn't wear those clothes back to Cite Soleil. It had been a while since she was back there and she needed to fit in when she returned. The one thing that Jean Paul always did when he brought a new member to his house, he made sure that they stripped down and kept their clothes as a reminder of the way they came to him when he found them. He ordered the butler to retrieve Rosie's original clothes when she first came to the house. He made sure they were washed and kept in a separate closet. Rosie was told to wear those same clothes back to Cite Soleil so no one would suspect that she no longer belonged in that slum.

Rosie's job was to simply find out where Deon was being held and by which branch of the Haitian Posse. Cite Soleil brought so much pain and bad memories to Rosie. When she was young she never thought that she would make it out of there alive, but it was also nostalgic to her. Those people in the slum would share the little they had with her when she was hungry and they always made sure she was all right. Sometimes she smiled at the thought of the older women chasing after her to make sure she wasn't doing anything that she wasn't supposed to do. Rosie was looking forward to going back home.

Marie

The kidnapping of Deon in front of Jean Paul's house made it difficult for Marie to continue to see Reginald. Jean Paul feared that someone had found out where his wife lived, so he ordered four of his security men to stand watch at the house all the time and two more to accompany her wherever she went. Marie was growing sexually frustrated because she could no longer enjoy Reginald's long strokes. She wouldn't dare mess with the help because she knew that was ground for termination, in the sense of death. She yearned for Reginald's touch and her pussy started having contractions and pulsated to the point where she had to pull her vibrator out to take care of her business.

She was mad that Deon was kidnapped in front of her house, but her husband kept all his business affairs with Deon from her. He figured the less she knew, the better off she would be in any situation, and this situation was no different. Deon hadn't even met his wife yet. It was probably a smart move on his part to keep Deon away from his wife. She probably would've tried to undress him with her lustful eyes, causing friction between the two men. Marie probably wouldn't be able to handle herself around a man as attractive and powerful as Deon. She was still disappointed with the fact that her dick supply had been cut off, and there didn't seem to be any relief in sight. Jean Paul already had problems satisfying her, but now she knew she wasn't going to get anything more from him than he had delivered in the past, because he had too much to deal with. It was best to keep using her vibrator. She felt her husband's twelve-inch dick was a waste.

Marie hadn't mentioned the kidnapping incident that took place in front of her house, but Reginald seemed a little too eager to find out if her husband was okay, during a conversation she had with him while she snuck in the shower with the phone. He was a little too inquisitive about her husband and she wondered what the hell was wrong with him. "I told you I won't be able to see you for a while, but why do you keep asking if my husband is alright?" she said to him in a concerning tone. "I just want to make sure the reason you can't see me is not because he's suspicious of us," he said to her. "What does my husband being suspicious have to do with me not being able to see you for a while?" she asked. "I just want to make sure he's not," he said with a suspicious tingle in his voice. Marie had always made it a point to talk as little as possible about her husband whenever she was with Reginald, but he was always prying for information. She didn't like that.

There was too much risk involved with the calls to Reginald, so Marie decided that she wouldn't call Reginald for a while. She would have to accept her vibrator, silver bullet and rabbit as a source of sexual relief for now. She didn't want her husband to find out she was cheating on him from one of his workers. She at least had the decency to show him that much respect.

Welcome Back

Rosie returned to her place of birth to find that nothing had changed. The people who had been there since she was a little girl were still being held captive by poverty, poor health, illiteracy, malnutrition, diseases and contamination. Everyone was happy to see her come back. All the little boys who drooled over her as children were now members of the Haitian Posse who carried big guns around feeling some kind of weird sense of pride and power. While walking around greeting everybody, Rosie started to realize the limitations that Cite Soleil and the country's government had placed on the people of Cite Soleil. Those slums should have been torn down and the people should have been moved to more habitable grounds where they could have access to safe drinking water and a sanitized living atmosphere.

Rosie's heart ached each time she saw a careless child wandering around without knowing that their world was a rut and there was no bright future in being in Cite Soleil. She had heard about Big Toutou's efforts to help bring hope to the people of Cite Soleil, but those efforts were not evident on the surface. The people still struggled and their faces reeked of pain and hardship. She almost couldn't take it any longer, but she had a job to do. It was no big secret that Big Toutou didn't sit on any throne and he made sure that he made himself available to all the residents in Cite Soleil. Naturally, Rosie wanted to meet the man that she had heard so much about. Who was this powerful man who made it his mission to save the worst slum in Haiti? What was the purpose? Big Toutou was not living lavishly even though the rumors on the street had him sitting on millions of dollars. He lived in a shack like the rest of the inhabitants of Cite Soleil and he carried his gun around for protection.

Rosie was surprised when the charismatic man approached her and introduced himself as Big Toutou. He stood at 6ft 5 inches tall and weighed just a little over 210 pounds. He really wasn't big at all, but tall. He wasn't as menacing as the rumors on the street portrayed him to be. He was rather cordial and warm. Rosie didn't see a cold blooded killer. She saw a charismatic leader standing for change and hope in a community of despair and hopelessness. "Koman ou ye?" she said to him in her native tongue. "Mwen bien," he answered. They basically exchanged greetings and Rosie told him she was happy to make his acquaintance because she had heard so much about him. "We do what we have to do out here because the government can care less whether we live or die here," he told her with conviction. She saw a man who was afraid, afraid of losing hope and afraid of failure of not trying. He truly believed his cause was just and kidnapping the rich people of Haiti was going to solve the problems his community faced.

There were rumors of a torture chamber at Cite Soleil, but Rosie didn't know how to ask him about those rumors without offending him. All of a sudden, she forgot that she was a native daughter of the place. Everybody from Cite Soleil knew what happened in Cite Soleil stayed in Cite Soleil, and Rosie was expected to adhere to those rules. "I can see you have something on your mind that you want to ask me," he said to her in Creole. He was able to read people easily. She was surprised by his special ability. "Go ahead. I'm sure I've heard every possible rumor about me and this place," he said to her. Finally, she said it, "I hear you have a torture chamber, is that true?" He smiled and said to her, "Can you keep a secret?" "Sure," she responded. Big Toutou grabbed Rosie's hand and asked her to follow him down to a long corridor where he kept all his captives while awaiting their ransoms. The room was guarded by three armed young men while the captives played dominos. They were all in good health and there wasn't a bruise on them. Rosie was surprised to see that Big Toutou wasn't as barbaric as the rumors on the street and the media portrayed him to be.

"You're probably shocked because you expected to see something completely different, huh?" he said to her. She shook her head in agreement. "You see, I have a philosophy that I follow and my organization was born from that philosophy. I don't kidnap people to torture them. I kidnap them because there needs to be some balance in the distribution of wealth as well as education in this country. While those people you saw in there live in a mansion on a hill, we have people down here who go many days without eating a meal. Where's the balance in that? Those rich people don't give a damn about these poor children and the welfare of this country. All they care about is their pocket. Well, I'm teaching them to share," he told Rosie. She didn't know what to say, but she did want to get one thing clear. "How come the Haitian Posse has been claiming credit for all these violent acts against the kidnapping victims?" she asked Big Toutou. "I guess that's a fair question," he said to her before continuing to explain it to her, "Well, when I first started this organization, I had a philosophy and I trusted that every member of my organization believed in our philosophy, but as the money started coming in, they no longer saw the importance of taking care of their own people. Instead, they started filling up their own pockets and started committing heinous crimes in the name of my organization. The real Haitian Posse only kidnaps the people we know who take advantage of the ghetto without giving anything back to the ghetto. We don't randomly kidnap people because we want to collect a ransom, we don't follow those guidelines. However, we also can't stop former members who have defected from our camp from using our name in vain. I'm not one to dog anybody from my camp whether current or former member, but the man upstairs is the judge of all judge, so they'll have their day. I don't need a publicity campaign to advertise what I do. I have enough cops looking for me in the city that no publicity campaign can ever change the image that they have bestowed upon us."

Rosie left Cite Soleil that day with a sense of pride and a genuine feeling from Big Toutou. He wasn't the sinister, ruthless killer that most people and the media had made him out to be. She also didn't want to be too naïve to believe everything that Big Toutou dished out to her was the truth. "Maybe he had a torture chamber and he chose not to show it to her," she thought, but the sincerity in his voice was enough to convince her he was being honest and straight-up about everything.

A New Plan

Jean Paul never expected Rosie to come back to him to tell him that she didn't think the Haitian Posse was involved in the kidnapping, especially after they claimed it. He thought Big Toutou had managed to fool her, but he also knew that Rosie's street smart was the best of all the women in the house. She basically was raised by the streets. He chose to go with her gut feelings about what she told him, only because he knew the guy he spoke with on the phone was not Big Toutou. Now he had to formulate a new plan to deal with the kidnappers. He wanted to be ready, but he didn't know what to get ready for. Whatever was going to happen was going to happen, but he knew that the kidnappers had no plan to make the exchange in a publicly crowded place.

Jean Paul hired a helicopter to be on standby so he could have the upper hand on the gang. Whatever location they chose to do the exchange, they were going to face death from above. Jean Paul came up with a plan to have the helicopter hover over the site where the exchange was going to take place and the order was to kill everybody, except

Deon. Maribel and Nadege were sharp shooters who would be placed strategically in the helicopter, while Rosie delivered the money. The Hoodfellas will be waiting about a half mile away to chase any oncoming car in case things get out of hand. While Jean Paul was going over the detail of his plan, Tweak interjected and asked, "Can I see your phone?" "Why?" Jean Paul asked curiously. "Since the guy had been calling from a cell phone, I can probably trace the phone call and use my computer to find his exact location. The GPS systems on the phone will help me locate him," Tweak told him. "Jean Paul had no idea that Tweak was a technological geek. Much could've been done if he had gotten The Hoodfellas involved in his plans from the very beginning. In his effort to ensure the safe return of Deon, Jean Paul didn't realize the valuable resources he had in Tweak, Crusher, Cindy and Smitty.

Tweak never left home without his gadgets and he found out that the phones system in Haiti was far from being technologically advanced. However, the only problem was the fact that they had to wait until the man called him back in order for Tweak to trace the call. "Cell phones are far easier to trace nowadays because big brother wants to keep an eye on all of us," he told the crew as he set up a device on the back of Jean Paul's phone that would reveal the exact location of the kidnappers. "The only thing that I'm gonna need you to do is to ask the man to keep Deon on the phone the whole time while we ride to meet him. I have a program on my computer that would lead us to his exact location as long as we can keep him on the phone," Tweak told him.

The restless period had begun and the crew couldn't wait until the next day so they could go wipe out the whole Haitian Posse. Regardless of the news Rosie brought back about Big Toutou, Jean Paul and The Hoodfellas had planned on making an example out of The Haitian Posse. It would be the last time they tried to kidnap anybody from their camp. The crew tried as much as they could to keep their minds free and get mentally ready for war the next day. The women were in the back yard practicing their shots. It had been a long time since Nadege, Maribel, Rosie, and Evelyne shot their guns. They enjoyed the camaraderie they once shared when they were in the Dominican Republic while training together. The girls had not gone into battle to put all that training to work, but they were looking forward to taking out the Haitian Posse.

Jean Paul decided to call it a night early and urged everybody else to do the same. Sex was not an option as he didn't want anybody to be deterred from the objective of bringing Deon back alive the next day. All the guys walked to their suites to think about what was waiting for them the following day. Crusher was all smiles as he thought about the last time The Hoodfellas went to war together. He started thinking about the two fallen soldier from the crew and the strong bond they formed in prison. He started to reminisce about the time when he teased No Neck about not being able to wipe his ass after he took a dump because his arms were too big to reach far back enough to wipe his butt. Crusher and No Neck were the best of friends within the crew. Crusher slowly started to drift asleep as he recalled all the good memories of his friend, No Neck and how Crazy D fought so hard to make sure the crew stayed together.

In the other room, Tweak's vision of his boy Short Dawg was a lot more vivid. He used to love watching Short Dawg make mice of men twice his size. He watched Short Dawg rise to every occasion presented to him and came out victorious in almost every challenge he faced. It was Short Dawg who taught Tweak to accept who he was and his talent. Being a geek in the hood was not considered a good thing, but Short Dawg was always quick to highlight Tweak's strength instead of his weaknesses. He cherished intelligence over strength even though he was considered to be a strong man instead of an intelligent one. Tweak smiled as he plopped down on his pillow to drift away to sleep with good memories of his friend, Short Dawg.

Cindy had the hardest time falling asleep. All she could think about was the man who came to her rescue when she felt her life was coming to an end. Without Deon, Cindy would still be stuck at the Webster mansion in the underworld of prostitution with men that she didn't care to be with. Deon had breathed life into her again. He made her feel like a woman. He never treated her like a prostitute or made her feel ashamed of her past. He was kind to her and for that she would always be grateful. The thought of losing Deon in a foreign land forced a stream of tears down her face. She silently cried until her eyes were too tired to shed any more tears and fell asleep on a soaked pillow.

Jean Paul was worn out from worrying about Deon's safety for the last 30+ hours. The thing that bothered him most was the fact that he hadn't even had time to earn the trust of The Hoodfellas, and then Deon was kidnapped under his watch. He was tormented, but more importantly, he wanted to show his loyalty to Deon and the crew. He would pull al the stops and use all the available resources he had to make sure that Deon was returned alive. He put his business plans on the back burner, and he also understood that he couldn't blame Deon if he didn't want to go into business with him anymore. All his worries exhausted him to the point where he started snoring so loudly he almost woke up everyone in the mansion.

Time For Some Action

It was imperative that the plan to rescue Deon was carried out accordingly. Everyone was once again briefed as they sat around the table to eat a traditional Haitian breakfast consisted of cornmeal cooked like grits and fresh slices of avocado with freshly squeezed orange juice. The reason why Jean Paul decided to have the traditional cornmeal was because most Haitians believe it gives them strength and energy. And the crew needed all the strength and energy they could muster because they had no idea what was waiting on the other side. The crew was still sitting at the breakfast table when they received the call for the drop-off location. "There's been a change in the plans," the man said to Jean Paul on the phone. Tweak ran to his room to get his computer so he can activate the electronic device to trace the call. Using an interconnection to Google map, he urged Jean Paul to extend the conversation with the man and to slow down his speech to give him enough time to get the device activated. "What do you mean there's been a change in the plans?" Jean Paul asked the man with curiosity. The man wanted so badly to increase the demanding price; he figured Jean Paul have no choice but to accept his offer. "After conferring with my partners, we decided that we can only release him for $200,000.00," the man revealed. "Who are you again?" Jean Paul asked in an effort to trip the man up. He knew it was the same person who talked to him the other day who wanted to act like he was Big Toutou. "Who me? I'm Maxo, Big Toutou's right hand man." The man lied. Jean Paul knew there was some kind of double-cross going on, but he wasn't sure who was playing whom.

The crew listened intently as Jean Paul continued his conversation with the man on the phone. However, they understood nothing as the conversation was in Creole. Jean Paul grabbed a pen and pad to take notes and tried his best not to rock the boat. "Listen, you're springing something on me I didn't anticipate. We had a deal at $100,000.00, but now you have doubled your price. I'm gonna need a little more time to come with that much more money," Jean Paul told him. "One more thing, if Deon has any broken bones or any serious bruises on him, the deal is dead," Jean Paul told him firmly. The man was surprised that Jean Paul had made that threat. "You're telling me what you want now? How about I go back there and put five bullets in his ass, huh?" the man threatened. It was a good thing that Jean Paul was speaking Creole because The Hoodfellas probably would've jumped on the phone and jeopardized Deon's life with more threats directed at the man. "Are you a business man? A businessman is about his money, not hurting people. I want to make sure that you don't hurt the man so you can get your money," Jean Paul told him.

While Jean Paul was on the phone, Tweak gave him the thumbs up as he was able to gauge the man's exact location. Jean Paul signaled with his hand to get the helicopter ready while he was still engaged in the conversation with the man. "Look you're gonna get your money and everything will be fine," he told the man. "I will call you back in exactly one hour," the man said before hanging up the phone.

Tweak was able to pinpoint that the phone call was made from a slum located in Bel Air. The whole crew scrambled to get their bullet proof vests and guns ready before they hopped in the helicopter that was sitting idle in the backyard, waiting on them. Tweak handed the pilot the address where they wanted to go and the rescue mission began. "Look, they're most likely gonna be driving the truck they hijacked from us. That's the truck we're gonna follow. I want Crusher, Smitty and Nadege to get on the three Ninja bikes I have in the garage. You guys ride, right?" Crusher and Smitty both shook their heads to confirm they were riders. "Nadege is fierce on the bike, so y'all need to follow her because she knows how to get to Bel Air quick and in a hurry," Jean Paul told them before they left the house. "We have special helmets that will allow all three of you to communicate with each other while riding, but Nadege will be the only one that can communicate with me while I'm in the helicopter. I need you all to wait for my order before you make any moves, clear?" It was hard for them to take orders from a man who wasn't their leader, but they had no choice. Jean Paul had to take charge of the situation because they were in his country.

Jean Paul, Tweak, Maribel and Cindy hopped in the helicopter while Nadege, Crusher and Smitty headed out on their motorcycles. Smitty was a stunt rider since he was twelve years old. He had no problem handling a Ninja bike. Crusher was a member of the Nasty Boys bike crew in Boston, his skills on a motorcycle was unmatched. Without too much time to put together a solid plan, Jean Paul was forced to improvise. The only money he brought with him was the 100 grand he planned on burning to celebrate the rescue mission, and burning every single member of the Haitian Posse alive was his goal. As the helicopter hovered in the sky in the direction of Bel Air, Jean Paul received a phone call from none other than Big Toutou himself. "Hello, who's this?" he asked. "This is Big Toutou. I understand that you have a situation and some people are trying to capitalize on my reputation and the reputation of my organization. I think we should talk," he told Jean Paul. "I'm really not in a position to talk right now, but we can definitely meet tomorrow," Jean Paul told him. "Look, I don't want you to be haste in your plans. I already know what's going down and I wanna help. You can call off your team and I can meet you at your house. We'll still have time to rescue your friend," Big Toutou told him. Jean Paul was shocked that Big Toutou even mentioned his house. He didn't think that people knew his private abode. "Okay. Meet me at my house in an hour," Jean Paul told him. Jean Paul quickly placed a call to Nadege to tell her to head back to the house with the crew.

Jean Paul was baffled by many things that Big Toutou said to him, he wasn't about to let his guard down. He warned his security forces to keep arm on Big Toutou from the time his helicopter landed in the backyard. He didn't know if Big Toutou had some tricks up his sleeve and didn't want to risk it. The members of The Hoodfellas also stood guard and armed in case Big Toutou wanted to try something funny.

The Big Picture

Big Toutou was also riding around in a helicopter. Many people in Haiti wondered how this guy was able to get around without being seen or caught by the cops. Big Toutou never set out to kidnap rich people in Haiti for personal gains. His original plan was to help the people of Cite Soleil and ensure that those children received the same opportunities to an education as those rich white and mullato kids who lived on the hill. He never deviated from his plan. However, some of the members of his camp started to get greedy. They wanted the big mansion on the hill and the lifestyle that these rich people were living. Greed and envy are the two most dangerous traits that a man can possess, Big Toutou learned. And it didn't take long for Big Toutou to figure out that Antoine was an envious and greedy man.

Each time they would hit a big score, Antoine always suggested they took the money and moved out of Cite Soleil. His vision and direction had become very different from the original philosophy that the Haitian Posse was found on. Big Toutou always wanted to live among the people in order to make them believe that his cause was about them. He wanted to prove he believed in them as people. He never cared about a big house, a car and a bunch of women. He wanted to offer people a better life, even if he was the last remaining person at Cite Soleil. From the time his organization was formed, he had sent almost 200 disadvantaged children to school with their tuition paid in full. He also made sure they received a meal when they got home from school. Most of those kids no longer lived in Cite Soleil as he had moved them to a better place in a complex that he was building under the name of a corporation in a town called, Tabar, located about thirty miles from Port Au Prince. The project would take some time to be completed, but every single family in Cite Soleil was guaranteed an apartment once it was done.

Big Toutou's plan was to move every single family out of the filthy slums of Cite Soleil slowly but surely, but he didn't want to draw any attention from the local police and the corrupted government officials. Every dime he had collected from the kidnappings went straight to the new complex he built in Tabar and an educational fund for the children he had moved from Cite Soleil to Tabar. The Haitian government made it easy for the children to be moved around because they don't have a record keeping system to track them in school or anywhere in the country. Also, Big Toutou was not just moving children, he was moving families. The 100-acre parcel of land Big Toutou purchased to build the facility he called The Hope and Dream complex, so he could move the families from Cite Soleil, was registered under a company he created in the name of his mother and his two sisters. They were the face of the project and nobody knew that they were related to Big Toutou. Those who knew kept it a well-known secret among themselves because Big Toutou was only trying to improve their lives. Loyalty ran deep in the slums of Cite Soleil. They were one of the first families to move into the complex. The buildings were being built slowly and the amenities would be the last focal point of the project. The land was slated to have about two hundred buildings consisting of one hundred two-bedroom apartments each. The project required a lot of money and Big Toutou knew that there was enough money in Haiti to make it happen. He just had to find a way to force the rich people of Haiti to contribute to his project.

Big Toutou's plan was to erect two hundred buildings consisting of a total number of fifty two-bedroom apartments each, a tutoring hall, cafeteria, sports facility, and recreation room to house a total number of ten thousand families. He had big dreams, but Big Toutou wasn't just a dreamer. He was also a doer. He found ways to get things done when people doubted him. While the kidnappings drew negative attention for Big Toutou and the Haitian Posse, he also found other ways to establish legitimate nonprofit organizations to help the homeless people of Haiti. He built a homeless shelter in La Plaine and made plans to build even more in every small province in Haiti. The charitable donations Big Toutou received for his nonprofit organizations had been the main source of financial support for most of his endeavors. Most of the money came from Haitians abroad and the rest from the generous business people in Haiti.

Big Toutou was no dummy. Every single one of his victims was targeted because they had shown no compassion towards the poor and disadvantaged; most of the time, these people had abused people or used their affluent position to mistreat them. There was a long list of millionaires on Big Toutou's list, and they all knew they were on his list. Some were bold enough to take the streets of Port Au Prince without security, while others took to the street with hired armed security. Big Toutou's men were always on the hunt for them. The fact that Big Toutou even forced them to give people jobs as security was satisfying to him. Sharing of the wealth was the most important thing.

Big Toutou also had a list of well-known philanthropists in Haiti. Those people who provided financial assistance to the legitimate nonprofit organizations in Haiti were protected and left alone by the Haitian Posse. Even anonymous donors were protected. Big Toutou was an informational genius. He had information on everybody. Jean Paul was never a target for him because of all the good deeds he had done since he came back to Haiti. Big Toutou paid close attention to him when he first moved back. At first, Big Toutou thought Jean Paul was gonna turn out to be another bloodsucker trying to suck the ghetto dry, but he found out soon enough that Jean Paul wanted to help the community and the less fortunate.

When his founding partner, Antoine, started to become selfish, Big Toutou simply asked him to go start his own organization with his own agenda, under his own organization name. However, since the Haitian Posse was known and feared, Antoine decided to move his regime to the Bel Air side of town and took on a completely different operation under the umbrella of the Haitian Posse.

A Game of Chess

Big Toutou wasn't a killer at heart, but he understood that sometimes it might be necessary to eliminate a few bad apples. And the worst apple of them all was his former friend and partner, Antoine Pierre Louis, the former Tonton Macoute. Big Toutou had never killed or abused anyone since the inception of the Haitian Posse. All of his victims had always been treated fairly and properly. His only motivation was the money. He never wanted to hurt anyone and he never did. However, because of the fact the Haitian Posse kidnapped its victims at gunpoint, Big Toutou was given the reputation of a monster. Many of his former victims have also fabricated tales of pain and maltreatment while under his custody. Since fear worked better than asking the rich people to help assist with the welfare of the poor people in Cite Soleil, Big Toutou decided to play on their fear. He never came out to publicly deny that he had ever hurt anyone. The rumors had created a reputation that preceded him.

Unfortunately, while Big Toutou allowed the myth that he was a monster to linger, his partner, Antoine, wanted to make it a reality. Antoine no longer shared the values of the Haitian Posse. He was ready to walk away and be on his own. He did just that, but in the process he has had Big Toutou under the guise of every big politician and police chief in Haiti. Antoine started recruiting hungry, hardcore criminal deportees from the minute they landed in Haiti to join his organization. He also went after former Tonton Macoutes that he knew were toxic enough to kill at will for no reason. His plan was working while destroying the original mission of the Haitian Posse.

Antoine embarked on a new plan to capture and kidnap rich people of any kind, regardless of their community involvement and philanthropy status. All he saw was green and he wanted it at all cost. The Haitian Posse went from a nonviolent group to the most violent gang in Port Au Prince. Antoine and his henchmen were going into people's homes in the middle of the night to kidnap them. His crimes were heinous and the rich people feared the organization completely. Quite a few of the people Big Toutou had kidnapped in the past continued to make donations to his organizations after they were released, but all that stopped when Antoine started to torture, rape and kill people in the name of the Haitian Posse. There had been instances where he decapitated people and mailed the head in a box to their family because they failed to pay his commanded ransom.

There was one particular case where Antoine and his men brutally raped the wife and killed the young daughter of a businessman because the businessman was an hour late with his ransom money. He had grown mad and angry and took out his frustration on the man's family. The lady's naked, and brutally beaten body, and her six year-old daughter's violated corpse were handed over to the husband who vowed revenge for his wife and daughter. Antoine knew that there had been a price on his head. Whenever Big Toutou reached out to him to try to get him to stop with his antics, he lied and told him that the people were exaggerating the same way they exaggerated him on the streets.

Big Toutou always stayed one step ahead of Antoine. He knew his whereabouts and all his involvements. He had wanted to take out Antoine for a while, but it was not in him to kill another human being. That was until he learned of the brutal rape of the woman and the murder of her child. Big Toutou vowed to put a stop to Antoine. He even turned down a high six figure offer from the woman's husband because he wanted to stop the train wreck right dead its track.

Big Toutou also maintained a cordial relationship with Antoine. He knew that an envious man like Antoine required extra precaution when dealing with him. Big Toutou would often call him just to stroke his ego, to make him feel like he's the man. And Antoine would always suck it all in. "You got these rich folks running for their lives. They're really afraid to come out of their homes. I never thought that our organization would have this much impact on the country, but you did it," Big Toutou told Antoine during a phone conversation, giving him full credit for everything. "Yes man, I know. These people respect me, I mean us, now. They can't drive around in their frosty Range Rovers without the fear of one us rolling up on them to kidnap them. That's powerful, man," he said to Big Toutou. He couldn't believe how this man was tripping on the phone over power. Big Toutou knew that the opportunity to take Antoine out would present itself one day and he didn't plan to miss it.

Big Toutou was angry at the fact that Antoine used his power, madness and insanity to turn a bunch of young men to cold blooded killers. These young men were supposed to get their second shot in life, but instead, he unraveled a world of violence, pain, strife and no hope on these young men. For that he needed to pay with his life.

Antoine managed to get the mansion on the hill that he wanted, but he was a prisoner in his own home. He required around the clock security and he was constantly shooting members of his own security team because of mistrust. His paranoia almost drove him insane to the point where he felt the whole world was after him. His stronghold was in the slums of Bel Air. He was able to sell a pipe dream to many of his soldiers and dissention in his camp was also becoming a problem. He used intimidation and violence to instill fear not just in his victims, but also his crew. Many of them didn't want to be part of his crew anymore, but they were too afraid to leave. His right hand man, nicknamed, 'Groneg," translated in English to "Big Man," because of his humongous, muscular frame, was a flunky and the most calculated killer of the crew. The man enjoyed killing people for no reason. He was a deportee who served fifteen years at Sing Sing penitentiary for murder before he was deported to Haiti. The man was completely demented and needed psychological help, but instead he encountered another psychopath who helped induce his appetite for killing. His iron fist approach of leadership kept a few of his soldiers in line, but many of them felt like they were prisoners all over again, and were willing to take their chances whenever the opportunity presented itself.

The Meeting

Big Toutou's helicopter landed about forty-five minutes later in the backyard of Jean Paul's house. Jean Paul was surprised to see this tall man with a muscular, but slim build and calm posture wearing a pair of blue denim jeans and a polo shirt, stepped out of the helicopter. Big Toutou was not a threatening looking man at all. "How ya doing?" he said, extending his arm to greet Jean Paul. "I'm fine. What's up?" Jean Paul said with an attitude trying to gauge Big Toutou's motive for coming to see him. "How the hell do you know where I live?" he asked Big Toutou curiously. "I know everything, man. I knew you sent Rosie to Cite Soleil to find out if I was the man behind the kidnapping of your friend. I have information officers everywhere, bro," he said confidently. Meanwhile, all the security men, the women and The Hoodfellas are standing guard with their guns in their hands. A few of them kept watch on the helicopter while the rest focused on Big Toutou.

It was enough of the small talk; Jean Paul wanted to know how Big Toutou was going to help him. Big Toutou chose to converse with Jean Paul in English because he didn't want his guests to feel left out. "Here's the situation, you're after a man that have left me no choice but to kill him. I'm not an assassin, but I'm willing to kill for the first time in my life because this man deserves it. It's not going to be easy for you to negotiate the release of your friend without my help, and that is why I'm going to need you to trust me, my friend," Big Toutou was calm and collected. "This guy's not even a killer!" Smitty yelled at the top of his lung making sure everyone had his attention. "Fuck that! We ain't gonna trust him with Deon's life on the line. We don't even know if this fool can pull the trigger. Hell naw!" he said while gripping his gun tightly in Big Toutou's direction. "I see you have an overly enthused soldier in your camp who wants nothing more than to prove his toughness," Big Toutou said to Jean Paul. "I suggest you tell him to calm the hell down because he can be eaten alive in a country like Haiti. We do things differently down here. This is the land of real killers where people don't give a goddamn even about a baby. He reminds me of a former friend," Big Toutou told Jean Paul. "He's just a little emotional about his friend being held captive. That's understandable," Jean Paul assured him. "Anyway, I wanted you to give me a chance to bring your friend back to you, but I am going to need your assistance in wiping out that whole gang," Big Toutou asked humbly. "Whatever you need, you just say it. We have manpower, guns, money, you name it," Jean Paul told him. "At this point the manpower and your guns are what's most important. I can't risk the lives of my men because this is not my war. I'm only trying to help you get rid of the trash. You see, Antoine is a coward and cowards like him only feel safe when they're surrounded by an army. So I know he's going to bring most of his trusted men with him to pick up the money from me in exchange for your friend. What I need you to do is to have your men and women stationed in the area so we can ambush his whole clan and wipe them off the face of the earth. The one favor that I ask is that you leave Antoine for me to kill," Big Toutou said calmly.

Jean Paul thought it was a fair enough deal. The two of them shook hands and Big Toutou started walking back to his helicopter. Before boarding the helicopter he turned to say, "I will call you in about an hour with the final plans." Jean Paul was ready and the crew was excited about going to war with Antoine and his men. The only thing they worried about was Deon's safety in the midst of gun battle.

The Follow-up

Big Toutou called back an hour later, as promised. The crew waited anxiously to hear some good news from Big Toutou. Jean Paul placed the call on speaker so the whole crew could hear the conversation. "I spoke with Antoine and I made it clear to him that I needed a favor from him on this particular case because the man he captured was a friend of a friend. He agreed to let me take Deon with me, but it's gonna cost two hundred and fifty thousand dollars," Jean Paul interjected to say, "He told me two hundred thousand earlier." "Jean Paul, I'm sure you know you're not dealing with an honorable man here. This man has no ethics and his only focus is the money. However, I will be a dead man before Antoine walk away with a dime of anybody's money ever again. I'm gonna need you to bring the money with you, but he's not leaving with it," Big Toutou assured him. "So, how we gonna do this?" Jean Paul asked anxiously. Big Toutou paused for a minute before he went into the details of his plan with Jean Paul and the crew.

Everybody was excited knowing that payback was only a couple of hours from their grasp. The same crew consisting of Nadege, Crusher and Smitty got back on their Ninja bikes to make their way down to a little town called Titanyen, which was about a couple hours away from Jacmel The three of them were ordered to stay about a mile away from the drop-off location on the outskirts of town until they heard the helicopter hovering above. Jean Paul wanted to make sure they were positioned just right for an ambush. The order was to annihilate the whole crew that Antoine brought with him, and no one was to be left alive under any circumstances. Big Toutou wanted to make sure that any member of Antoine's clan who stayed behind would be scared enough to go into hiding and never regroup as a gang. Smitty's weapon of choice was an automatic Uzi with 32 shells. He brought four extra clips in case he ran out of ammo. Nadege carried two baby 9's and six clips of ammunition. Crusher was a big man, so he opted for .12-gauge sawed off shot gun and a .45 Lugar with enough ammo to fight an army. The rest of the crew loaded the helicopter with grenade launchers, machine gun, bazooka, AK-47's and dynamite. They were ready for war. Cindy was so amped up about rescuing her man that Maribel was laughing at her.

As the helicopter hovered over the blue skies of Haiti, Jean Paul thought about the possibility of casualties among the group. He silently said a prayer to himself for the group asking God to watch over them and make sure they all return in one piece. He understood whenever someone engaged in a war, there was always a probability of casualties. The bullet proof vest only protected their chests and nothing else. He looked around in the helicopter to see a group of loyal friends willing to risk their lives for the life of one man. He had started to believe that that type of loyalty didn't exist anymore.

Action!

The pilot could see the armed men on the open field as he approached the drop-off point. They scoured all over the place and their location was easily noticeable. Everyone moved to the back of the helicopter to avoid being spotted by Antoine and his men. Antoine trusted that Big Toutou would stick to his word and have the people drop off the money and the ordeal would be over. This time he was wrong. Antoine had gone too far and it was getting out of control. Big Toutou needed to put a stop to Antoine's antics quickly before most of the streets of Haiti turned bloody. Antoine had taken away the civility of Big Toutou's movement and it was time for him to pay. Antoine also agreed to return the Toyota Sequoia truck as part of the deal even though he knew that it was the best weapon in his possession. A bullet proof car is even better than a gun in a battle.

The Sequoia was parked between two trucks, one in the front and one in the back loaded with armed men. There was hardly any space between the three cars for any movement. The Sequoia could not go anywhere. Big Toutou sat behind the wheel of the beat-up Nissan, Pathfinder truck parked in the front, while Deon sat in the front passenger seat. Big Toutou's phone was taken away and he had no way to inform Jean Paul of the last minute changes in the plans.

Antoine and two armed men sat in the Sequoia, And behind them in a Mitsubishi, Montero truck, sat four armed gun men ready to take out anybody who crossed their path. Antoine's words have never been true and Big Toutou thought he had gained his trust enough to make the deal happen. Antoine switched the plans at the last minute. He decided he was going to keep the Sequoia and kill both, Deon and Big Toutou so he could be the sole leader of the Haitian Posse. Big Toutou had no way of making contact with Jean Paul, he was doomed.

The plan was for the helicopter to open fire on the other two trucks killing everyone inside after they drove away from the Sequoia. Big Toutou and Deon were supposed be sitting in the Sequoia and would drive off after the money is collected. The tinted windows on the cars made it hard for Jean Paul and his crew to see who was sitting in what car. Jean Paul and The Hoodfellas could exterminate everyone except the man that they wanted to kill. Something had to be done.

Big Toutou looked over to see the horror carved onto Deon's bruised face. His beaten-body made him appear as if he were in a surrendering state. The brutal treatment he had undergone the last couple of days under the hand of Antoine would never leave his memory. He could not walk away from the situation without having the satisfaction of killing Antoine himself. He could hardly sit up, and his eyes were swollen shut from the repeated blows that Antoine personally delivered to his face. Antoine had never met a man that he couldn't break down and Deon wasn't about to help him maintain a perfect streak. The daily torture Deon received so he could reveal to Antoine the reason he was Haiti was worst than the torture the prisoners at Abu Ghraib prison in Iraq received at the hands of the United States army.

The thirst for revenge was written on Crazy D's face. By then the metamorphosis had already taken place. Deon was long gone and Crazy D had taken over. Crazy D and Big Toutou hadn't shared many words, but Big Toutou tried to apologize to him for the physical torture Antoine administered on him. Neither men were armed, but they waited patiently as one bag of money was dropped off from the helicopter. Antoine sent one of his men to retrieve the bag to make sure that the content of the bag was half of the money he was promised. After securing the first bag, which contained half off the money, the truck behind the Sequoia pulled away from it, while the one in the front remained still. Antoine had told Big Toutou not to pull away in the truck until the second bag of money was dropped off.

The silence in the car was nerving wracking. Big Toutou knew there was only two ways out of the situation. Since Antoine had changed the plans on him in the last minutes, he knew there was no way Antoine was going to let them live. He also knew that their lives were in jeopardy at the hands of Jean Paul and his men. The plan was for Jean Paul's crew to open fire on every car except for the Sequoia. Before facing his death, Big Toutou wanted to at least tell Crazy D how his friends cared so much about him. "I know we may not make it outta here alive, but you need to know that you got some great friends out there and they care about you greatly. I'm sorry about your experience in Haiti," Big Toutou told him before accepting his fate as a dead man breathing. Big Toutou also told Crazy D a little about his dealings in Haiti and his big dreams to revamp the children of the ghetto. Inside, Crazy D was proud of this stranger he had befriended in possible death. Big Toutou may have resigned to his possible death, but Crazy D was not ready to die yet. He had too much to live for. He thought about his responsibility to The Hoodfellas he brought to Haiti with him, the fact that he hadn't avenged Short Dawg and No Neck's deaths, and he hadn't reconnected with his mother, and most of all, live life.

"I ain't going out like that," Crazy D finally spoke to Big Toutou. "What should we do?" Big Toutou asked. "The windows are tinted and the car runs, right?" Crazy D asked. Big Toutou shook his head to confirm. "Well, they can only see us from the front. If you put the petal to the metal and keep our heads down, that would signal to my team that the plans have gone haywire and we might have a chance, instead of just sitting here waiting to die," Crazy D told him. "I got you. Let's do this!" Big Toutou said excitedly about his chances of survival. "Ok, on 3, put the car in drive and floor this bad boy," Crazy D told him. Big Toutou put the car in drive after counting to 3 and they took off across the rough terrain with their heads down on the seat and no hand on the wheel. Gun fire erupted towards the Nissan. Jean Paul and The Hoodfellas knew that Crazy D and Big Toutou had to be in the Nissan because Antoine's men were aiming and shooting at it while the Sequoia and the Montero chased it. Crazy D and Big Toutou where headed to nowhere, but Big Toutou kept his foot on the gas. In the process, they ran over a couple of men who tried to be heroes by standing in front of the truck, shooting.

The military style helicopter pulled out of range to avoid gunfire, as everyone inside emerged with guns in hands, shooting at everything in sight on the ground, except for the Nissan. While manning the machine gun, Tweak blew the lid off the hood of the Montero in pursuit of the Nissan. Jean Paul called Nadege to tell her that there had been a switch in the car of interest and they were to protect the Nissan, Pathfinder. All three motorcycles emerged from the distance with gun fire coming from three different directions toward Antoine's crew. Young Smitty was like a stunt man as he stood on his bike, while unloading his automatic Uzi killing every man in his path. Crusher was more up close and personal as he weaved in the crowd of men shooting at point blank range dropping as many men in sight as possible. Nadege was sitting on the end of her bike with her back to the handle bar while emptying clips of nine millimeter hollow bullets into bodies, dropping men like she was at a shooting range. Antoine and his team didn't know what was in store for them.

The members who decided to defect in the middle of hailing bullets were killed in their cowardice state. Maribel lit up a stick of dynamite and dropped it on a group of five men whose limbs blew into pieces splattering all over the place. Meanwhile, Antoine and the boys in the Sequoia decided to run away from enemy fire and took to the streets to head to Port Au Prince. Crazy D wanted to give chase, but not without grabbing the grenade launcher and the bazooka from Jean Paul in the helicopter. While Big Toutou whipped the Pathfinder, Crazy D sat on the door through the window and launched a grenade at the Sequoia. The first one missed and exploded on the ground on the path in front of the truck, forcing the driver to make a U-turn. He had no idea where the explosion was coming from. Crazy D reloaded the launcher and let loose another grenade that hit the bottom back of the Sequoia forcing it to flip over. The Nissan stopped and Big Toutou and Crazy D got out of the Nissan and started moving towards the Sequoia. Crazy D was on one side of the Sequoia holding the grenade launcher in his hands while Big Toutou knelt down on one knee on the other side of the truck with the bazooka over his shoulder.

Antoine had lost control of the situation and any wrong move could cause him to have his spleen and brains splattered yards apart on the hot pavement. He contemplated his next move, but there was really nothing to contemplate. As he and his men exited the upside down truck, Smitty pulled up on the bike and unload his Uzi killing every single man before they could even get back on their feet. Seeing this, Antoine quickly retrieved back into the truck. His right hand man, Groneg, was on his stomach trying to crawl back towards the truck, but Smitty also helped put an end to his misery by unloading a round of shots in his back.

Antoine allowed the bitch within to take over and he refused to exit the Sequoia. Smitty also wanted to help him make up his mind, but Crazy D quickly signaled for him to stop. "Get the fuck out of the truck or I will blow it to pieces with you in it," Big Toutou screamed in Creole confusing the hell out of Crazy D, before repeating it again in English. Big Toutou was out to kill and he wanted Antoine to suffer. "Come out here and face death like man, you coward. All those people you killed never had a chance. At least I'm giving you a chance to be a man before you die," Big Toutou told him. Crazy turned to Big Toutou and said, "Look bro, I don't know what the fuck you're saying, but you sound like you're pissed, and I understand that. However, I think I deserve to do him in more than you. Look at me bro, I look like a monster because of this man," Crazy D said while pointing to his face. While Big Toutou and Crazy D were fighting over who had the right to kill Antoine, he snuck out of the truck with a gun in his hand aiming to kill both of them. Unfortunately, he wasn't a quick enough shot because trigger happy Smitty was standing in front of him with the gun in his hand as Antoine aimed to shoot. When Big Toutou and Crazy D heard a hail of bullets sounding off before Antoine dropped to the ground, they both looked to Smitty and said, "Goddddddddddddddamn!" in unison. However, Smitty shook his head to say he wasn't the one who shot Antoine. Cindy let loose a succession of shots from her automatic 9mm glock in the back of Antoine's head from the other side, making it sound like it was a machine gun unloading. She was getting her man home one way or another.

Big Toutou, Cindy and Crazy D were about to walk away to join the rest of the crew back where they were tying up the loose ends with possible survivors when Smitty yelled, "Boss! You forgot to take the money out the truck." The adrenaline of rush of the situation caused Crazy D to completely forget about the money. He already knew his plans for that money. As much as Jean Paul wanted to burn every member of Antoine's crew with the money, Crazy D found a better way to put the money to good use. He looked toward his new friend, Big Toutou, handed him the bag of money and said "This is for the children of the slum of Cite Soleil. You can pick up the other half when we get to the helicopter." Big Toutou was grateful as he opened his arms to hug his new friend.

Meanwhile Maribel, Nadege, Tweak, Crusher, Cindy and Jean Paul shot every single member of Antoine's crew execution style even after they laid down their guns. Gasoline was doused on them and they were all burned to hell. They wanted to send a message to anybody who had any inclination of ever messing with The Hoodfellas and Jean Paul in Haiti again. All the men gathered around the Sequoia and together they flipped it back up so Maribel could drive it back to the mansion, following Smitty, Nadege and Crusher on their bikes. There was no need to clean up the mess because Jean Paul knew that the police was gonna blame the bloody mess on gang warfare. Big Toutou was dropped off to an undisclosed location, while the crew returned back to the mansion in Jacmel with their prize and leader.

A New Day

Crazy D was happy that he was rescued from Antoine's gang, but he was bothered by the fact that Antoine knew how to get to Jean Paul so easily. He felt there was a leak somewhere in Jean Paul's organization and he had better gotten to the bottom of it before Jean Paul was kidnapped in Haiti by another gang looking for a big score. Antoine's crew wasn't the only gang in Haiti kidnapping people and torturing them in the name of the Haitian Posse. There were many other copycat gangs all over Port Au Prince. While Jean Paul and everyone else in the house urged Deon to relax so he could recuperate from his injuries, he refused to do it. There was a problem and he felt a solution was imminent because he didn't feel safe as long as there was a mole amongst them.

Maribel allowed Cindy to spend the first night with Deon when he came back, but she couldn't wait to help nurse him back to his old self. Whenever she thought about the bravery that Deon displayed through the ordeal, her panties got wet. She knew that he was the type of man she wanted to be with and she didn't mind sharing him with

Cindy. Jean Paul didn't even trip when he noticed that Maribel was latching on to Deon. There were many more Maribels to come and he was more than happy to set her free to find happiness.

The crew celebrated the return of Deon by throwing him a party. Jean Paul had his maids prepare a grand fiesta to welcome his friend home. Food and drink were abundant. Fried pork aka Griot, fried beef aka Tasso, conch aka Lambi, fried chicken, fried plantain, rice and beans, macaroni salad, beet, marinade and akra filled the table as the crew sat down to feast on a grandiose meal especially catered for the occasion. "I'd like to make a toast," Jean Paul said as he raised his glass. "I'm thankful and grateful for the safe return of my friend Deon, and I'm also grateful for The Hoodfellas family as well as my own family here," he said as he pointed his glass around in the direction of the women and his staff. Everybody ate and drank until late that night. The Hoodfellas poured drinks out in the memory of the two fallen soldiers. At the end of the night, everybody linked up with their women for more sexual adventures. Jean Paul had two new bombshells brought to the house. They were training in the Dominican Republic for the last four weeks with the commander. However, he wanted to do a little training of his own after the party with the two of them.

Maribel couldn't wait to get a taste of big daddy and Cindy. Her pussy was pulsating as she looked over to Deon to see the outline of his long dick through his white linen pants. All she could do was lick her lips while he looked on. Cindy walked over and whispered, "I think Maribel wants us tonight, Daddy," in Deon's ear. Maribel ran her hands up and down her curvaceous body when he turned to look over to her. It was his cue to go to his suite to get some much needed loving.

Cindy worked slowly to remove the white linen shirt that kept hidden the chiseled frame that Deon worked relentlessly in prison to achieve. She ran her hands over his chest while she stood in front of him, and Maribel started caressing his back from behind. Deon's bruises had healed substantially under the care of Maribel and Cindy but he wasn't 100 percent yet. He positioned his hand on the back of Cindy's neck to give her a passionate kiss as Maribel told him, "We miss you, daddy." The drawstring on Deon's pants came untied so quickly he didn't even realize that they had dropped to his ankles. Maribel had reached around to pull the strings while Cindy kissed him. She started rubbing his dick through his underwear as his kiss with Cindy lingered. By then, the blood flow in Deon's pants was to a maximum and Maribel couldn't help herself as she squatted down to get a taste of his manhood.

The form fitting dress that Cindy wore rolled up above her thighs in no time as Deon started to palm what very little ass she has, and sucking on her breasts while he received a blowjob from Maribel. "Daddy, you feel so good," Cindy revealed through passionate whispers. A couple of his fingers soon made their way into Cindy's pussy and her wetness came flowing down. Cindy was hungry for Deon. He moved Maribel to the side, picked up Cindy and stuck his hardened dick inside her while he held her up against the wall. "Give it to me, daddy," she screamed in the middle of his strokes. "I want you to beg for this dick," he said to her. "I want your dick, daddy. Please give it to me," she begged almost nearing tears for having thoughts of him possibly being gone the past few days. Deon continued to stroke her as Maribel stood back to watch. Cindy wrapped her legs around Deon's body for support as she went up and down his dick until sweat started pouring all over them. Maribel by now was sitting on the bed masturbating to the scene in front of her. She couldn't wait to have some of Deon's dick. Cindy started to intensify her grinding as the tension from her body searched for relief. "Oh yes! Oh yes! I'm coming!" she started to scream. Deon never lost his stride as he fucked her until she held on tight to him as a stream of white cream exited her pussy.

After Cindy came, Maribel was still on the bed playing with her clit. Deon placed Cindy on the floor and moved towards the bed to give Maribel a helping hand. She was lying on her back and her legs were spread wide open across the bed as Deon slowly inserted his erect dick inside of her. "O yes, papi," she said as his dick filled her pussy. Deon pulled her towards him as he put his hands under her leg so he could stroke her to ecstasy. His rhythm was solid as he stroked and stroked and stroked Maribel. "I miss your dick, papi," she said through every stroke. Deon was working hard to make sure Maribel came. He started using his thumb to rub her clit while stroking her. The double sensation was too much for her to bear and within minutes she was yelling "Adios mios, you're making me cum, papi." Deon stroked her even harder until Maribel couldn't stand it anymore and allowed the secretion to exit her body.

Though Deon had just satisfied the two women, they sensed that something was bothering him. Deon had never been with them without reaching climax at least once. It felt like he wasn't into it for himself this time. "What's wrong baby?" Cindy asked. "Nothing really," he responded. "Are you sure? You don't seem like your normal self," Cindy told him. "I just need some rest. I'll probably feel a lot better in the morning. They all agreed. The three of them hopped in the king size bed and went to sleep.

Finding The Mole

Jean Paul was well aware of the fact that Deon was right about an existing mole within his camp. He had to figure out who it was, and once he found him, death would be the ultimate punishment. After talking to Big Toutou on the helicopter ride from the bloody massacre of Antoine's crew, Jean Paul learned that Big Toutou had more information on his organization than he thought. Big Toutou was aware of all his illegal dealings, but he understood that Jean Paul was also trying to help people seek a better life, which was one of the reasons The Haitian Posse never came after him. Jean Paul had no idea that Big Toutou was so well-connected. The helicopter he used to come to Jean Paul's house was courtesy of the businessman who promised to make every resource available to him to make sure Antoine paid with his life. Initially, the man wanted Antoine's decapitated head, but Big Toutou quickly convinced him that he didn't have to become as inhumane as Antoine's crew had become. Nevertheless, the businessman was happy that Antoine was killed. He felt that his little girl didn't die in vain.

Jean Paul also learned from Big Toutou that the hit was originally meant for him, not Deon. Jean Paul hardly took the wheel when he rode around Port Au Prince because he had a full-time driver. However, when the kidnappers opened the passenger side of the Sequoia, they thought it Jean Paul who was sitting in the passenger seat. Without thinking about it, they threw a bag over Deon's face shielding confirmation of his identity. It wasn't until they arrived at their camp that they realized they had kidnapped the wrong person. But it didn't matter to Antoine; he knew he could still get some kind of money out of the deal. Since he was unaware of Deon's financial status, he decided to cut his price down to 1% of the original asking price of 100 million dollars that he felt he would've gotten if he had captured Jean Paul. Allowing people in Haiti to think he was a billionaire almost cost Jean Paul his life because he damn sure didn't have 100 million dollars lying around to pay Antoine in case he had to. Antoine ended up shooting two of the men who brought him Deon instead of Jean Paul. He shot them at point blank range for their mistake.

Jean Paul understood that peace of mind cultivated great health and he had no peace of mind as long as the mole continued to be among his crew. He thought hard about who from his camp it could be that tried to set him up, but came up with nothing. All of his men had been with him since he moved to Haiti. And he knew that the women couldn't have done it because he had never discussed his traveling plans with them. He could find no logical person to weed out. The only other person who could've set him up was his wife, but she would never be that stupid or crazy. She loved the lifestyle he provided for her and he had never done her dirty. Besides, he always surprised her when he visited her in Thomassin. She didn't know when he was coming or going.

Racking his brain was not getting Jean Paul the answers he was looking for, so Jean Paul decided to call his wife to see how she was doing. "Hi baby," she said through the speaker of the phone when she heard her husband's voice. 'How are you? Is everything ok? I miss you," he said in succession. "I'm fine. Everything is ok and I miss you too. When are you coming to see me?" she asked him. "I'm not sure yet, but you will see me soon," he told her before hanging up the phone.

After getting off the phone with her, Jean Paul called one of his security men posted at his wife's house to check if everything was all good. "Gerard, sak pase? Tout bagay en fom?" he asked in Creole when the security guard picked up the cell phone. "Kijan'w ye, boss? Tout bagay en fom wi. Boss, mwen konin se pa biznis mwen, min mademoisel la te kite telefon li sou tab la, mwen te we ou messaj ak ou non Reginald ki tap flashe ladan'n pandan'l tap vibre wi. Messaj la di ke li manke mamzel. Mwen te vle di'w sa pou'w ka konin," the security guard said in Creole to Jean Paul. The information the security guard had just revealed to Jean Paul sent a sharp arrow right through his heart. "How could she be cheating on me?" he thought to himself. He provided her with everything a woman could want. He didn't know what to do. No man wants to reveal to another man that his wife has betrayed him. He thought long and hard about it and decided that maybe Deon might be able to help him come up with a solution to his problem.

It took a lot of courage for Jean Paul to even open himself to the possible ridicule he might face for allowing Deon to know the softer side of him. He knocked on Deon's door. "Yo, D, you got a minute?" he said through the door. "Who's this, JP?" Deon asked. "Yeah, it's me. When you get a minute, come downstairs to my office. I need to talk to you about something," Jean Paul told him before making his way downstairs to his office. Deon got up, put on his slippers, brushed his teeth and threw on his silk robe over his silk pajama to head down to Jean Paul's office.

He knocked on the door a couple of times before Jean Paul was awoken out of his trance and said, "Come in." Deon instantly knew something was bothering Jean Paul from his demeanor. "What's on your mind, JP?" he asked. Jean Paul took a long deep breath before he let the words escape his mouth, "Man, I think my wife is cheating on me." Why you say that?" Deon asked with curiosity. "I just spoke with one of my security men and he told me that my wife left her phone on the table to go use the bathroom, when the phone started vibrating he saw a text message from a man named Reginald saying he missed her. I give that fucking broad everything, man," he said with emotional sadness in his voice. "Man, you can't let no broad affect you like that, man. You got all these fine ass chicks in here that you handed over to me and my crew without even sweating it, but you're letting your wife affect you? If she's gonna go out on you, then that means she was never down with you. Take that posh lifestyle away from her and cut her ass loose. We're hustlers! We can't get all emotionally wrapped up in broads. She might be doing you a favor. See, I ain't never really been in love with no broad, but I can appreciate a broad who's down with me. You'll be aight, player. Put your foot down and let her know that you know what she's up to," Deon said to him. It wasn't exactly the comforting words that he was looking for, but Jean Paul knew that there was some validity to what Deon had said. Besides, it wasn't like he was faithful to her.

Taking Care of Business

After talking to Deon, Jean Paul got on the phone, called his security men to tell them to bring his wife to his condo in Jacmel right away. He also instructed them to take her phone away from her. He knew she could get feisty; he warned his men not to take her lightly. Jean Paul got himself dressed and drove to his condo located about five miles away from his house. He had never told his wife about the mansion. He led her to believe he lived in the three-bedroom condo suite located in the heart of Jacmel. When two of his men showed up to the door with Marie, they each held one of her arms. The evidence of her feistiness was all over their faces as she left scratch marks and streaks all over them. After they opened the door, he told them to let her go so she could enter the condo. The two men stood guard outside of the door while Jean Paul and his wife were inside conversing. A few seconds later, one of the security men knocked on the door to hand Marie's phone to Jean Paul. He also told him that Marie fought them hard trying to destroy the phone.

Jean Paul calmly made his way to the couch while his wife stood in the middle of the living room. "Who is he?" he asked her nonchalantly. "Who's who?" she answered him sarcastically. "Look, we're not gonna play games here because you know I don't have time to waste," he told her sternly. "You don't have time to waste because you gotta go over to your little mansion to fuck all those skeezers you got livin' in there with you?" She went on the offensive. Jean Paul thought his mansion was a hidden secret from his wife, when she knew all along knew what had been going from day one. "We're not here to talk about what I'm doing. I'm simply asking you a question about the man you're cheating behind my back with because my safety may be in jeopardy. Now, who the fuck is he?" he asked her with his voice raised, almost scaring her. "You think I wanted to cheat on you? I never wanted to do that to you, but I hardly see you and when I do see you, you're always ready to leave the minute I see you. I don't even wanna talk about our sex life, because it's nonexistent...." She started rambling on before he cut off said, "I'm not here to talk about me and you. Who the fuck is this man? I'm not gonna ask you again," in an even higher octave. The seriousness and anger coming from Jean Paul's voice almost scared the pants off Marie. "His name is Reginald. I met him at the bodyshop when I had that car accident I told you about," she said. "You told me about the accident, but you didn't tell me you were fucking him," Jean Paul said angrily. "Does this guy know anything about me? Does he know who I am?" he asked her, still with an angry tone. "I never told him anything about you, but I'm sure he figured out that you were a man of high status because of the car that I drove."

"Marie, or should I call you Sandra? Which do you prefer?" Her mouth almost dropped to the floor when Jean Paul threw the name Sandra in her face. She thought she had managed to keep her past a secret from him. Thanks to Big Toutou, Jean Paul learned of his wife's past and how she was deported to Haiti for drug possession. For the last few days after he talked to Big Toutou, he was afraid that his wife might've been the person to set him, but he didn't want The Hoodfellas to think that his operation was that hollow, which would've shown weakness on his part, so he said nothing. But he damn sure planned on finding out if she was behind Deon's kidnapping.

He took her phone and strolled down all the text messages she had been receiving from Reginald. "You and this guy had a love affair, huh?" he said facetiously. "I don't love him. I love you," she said with tears streaming down her face. "You love me so much you let another man stick his dick inside you. That's love, huh?" he said to her with sarcasm in his voice. Marie didn't really want to anger Jean Paul further, so she kept her mouth shut while he talked. As Jean Paul was rummaging through her phone looking for more text messages, Reginald sent her a new text telling her that his brother had been killed in a bloody gang shoot-out. He found that out on the news. The text drew interest from Jean Paul immediately. The only shoot-out that Jean Paul knew of that took place in Haiti, was the one he was involved with, a couple of days ago. "I'm sorry to hear that baby, how did he die?" Jean Paul text him back. "I don't know, but I need to see you. I have no money to bury him and I know it's gonna cost at least ten thousand dollars for a funeral. You think you can get the money from your husband to lend me?" he text back. "Sure. I'm sorry about your brother's death," Jean Paul text back trying to sound sincere.

Jean Paul was heated inside because he knew that Reginald was just using his wife. He wanted to pull his gun out and put a bullet in her head right there in the living room. A few minutes later, another text came through from Reginald. "You think you can sneak away so I can see you tonight to get the money?" he asked. "I'm gonna use an excuse to get away from the guards. I should have the money by 5:00 pm. Where do you want to meet?" Jean Paul text him back. It was important that Jean Paul told him that the money wouldn't be available until 5:00 pm because the drive from Jacmel to Port Au Prince was almost four hours. "We can meet at out favorite spot at 7:00," he text back moments later. Jean Paul didn't care to know about their favorite spot; he wanted to make sure he met Reginald where there was no crowd of people. "How about we meet at Le Lambi beach instead? There shouldn't be anybody there by that time. It'll be just the two of us. I can't wait to see you so I can give it to you, baby," Jean Paul text him back. "Wow, we never did it on the beach before. That sounds good. I'll see you at 7:00," he confirmed.

Jean Paul turned to look at Marie in disgust. "What the fuck else have you been lying to me about?" he asked her angrily without mentioning his plan to meet with Reginald later. She stayed quiet. She didn't want to answer his question. He opened the door and asked his security men to keep watch on her while he was gone. "Make sure she doesn't touch the phone or talk to anybody while I'm gone," he instructed his guards.

Jean Paul went back to the mansion to ask Deon and The Hoodfellas for assistance with the situation. After explaining the series of event to Deon and the crew, they were more than happy to help. With Nadege behind the wheel, Deon, Crusher, Smitty and Tweak piled into the bullet-proof seven-passenger Toyota, Land Cruiser that was sitting in the garage collecting dust, while Jean Paul led the way in his wife's Mercedes truck. Cindy, Maribel and Evelyne were told to wait at the house.

Jean Paul had no idea if Reginald was part of Antoine's gang or if he was just a loverboy rocking his wife's bed at night. He only wished that she had never brought the man to his house. He was thinking and visualizing all kinds of stupid sexual shit that his wife had done with Reginald. The anger in his eyes was enough to wipe out a town. He drove anxiously to Port Au Prince anticipating nothing less than the complete elimination of this man. He even thought about torturing the man for sleeping with his wife, but those thoughts quickly faded as he realized that a man could only get as far with a married woman as she allow him to go. He shifted the blame to his wife and settled on just killing the man.

Jean Paul asked the crew to fall back about a quarter of mile away from him. He sat in the darkly tinted windows Mercecdes, ML 350 truck waiting for Reginald. A few minutes later, a tan older model Nissan, Maxima, pulled into the parking lot and this bowlegged man appeared. Jean Paul looked around him and cocked his gun before he stepped out of the car to meet Reginald half the distance towards the car. The minute the car door swung open and Jean Paul stepped out, he was surrounded. A bunch of armed men came out of nowhere with automatic weapons and pointed them at him. He didn't stand a chance and laughter spread across Reginald's face. "Drop your fucking gun!" screamed one of the men to Jean Paul. The Hoodfellas were waiting on a cue from Jean Paul to move, but the horn from the Mercedes truck never sounded as planned, even after a few minutes since the Nissan, Maxima pulled into the parking lot. Deon sensed something was wrong, but he continued to stay put.

Reginald knew it was a set-up when Jean Paul suggested they meet at Le Lambi Beach. Marie was petrified of the beach because she almost drowned at the beach as a child. She shared that story with Reginald while they were lying in bed once at a hotel after hours of having passionate sex. He was hoping to kidnap Jean Paul himself to get the ransom that his brother lost his life for.

"You really think you were gonna get away with killing my brother?" Reginald asked Jean Paul. He wanted to smack the taste off Reginald's face, but he was being restrained by two of Reginald's men. Reginald tried to force an answer out of him by smacking him across the left side of his face. "You sure you wanna do this?" Jean Paul said with a devilish grin while licking the blood off his lips. A loud thundering sound reflected another smack landing to the right side of Jean Paul's face. "So you must be a gangster too," he said to Reginald. "Groneg was the only brother I ever knew and you took him away from me," Reginald told him before landing a punch to his gut. Jean Paul's mind was working a mile a minute as he tried to figure out the situation. He had heard the name Groneg before, but he wasn't sure where. "You're gonna pay with your life for killing my brother," Reginald told him before landing another blow to his chest.

Unfortunately, Reginald took a little too long with his soliloquy, as gunfire erupted from The Hoodfellas who grew impatient waiting for Jean Paul's signal. Reginald found himself dodging bullets and running for his life while three of his men dropped from shots fired by The Hoodfellas. Jean Paul tried to run back toward the Mercedes, but not before a bullet pierced through his back and exploded inside of him, leaving fragments that made it potentially impossible for him to survive. Deon ran towards him and got him inside the bullet-proof truck. He had already empty one clip of bullets on the automatic Uzi. He inserted another clip while using the car as a shield and men started dropping like flies as bullets went flying into their bodies. The bodies were falling all over the place as the gun battle ensued for another minute. By the time the gunfire stopped, Smitty, Crusher and Deon were the only people left standing.

Nadege and Tweak were both lying in a pool of blood with their eyes wide open and bullet holes all over their bodies. Everyone forgot to wear their protective bullet proof vest as rushed out of the house. They didn't anticipate a gun battle. As Crazy D emerged once again, he went around making sure that every wounded body lying on the ground was confirmed dead by unloading two clips of bullets in them. Reginald's face was almost unrecognizable as Deon and Smitty shot his face up with enough bullets to supply a whole police department.

As Smitty and Crusher piled the bodies of Nadege and Tweak in the truck, Deon felt a pulse coming from Tweak's arm. Jean Paul hadn't yet died but he was close to passing out. All Deon wanted was to make it to the hospital to give Tweak and Jean Paul a chance at survival. He had no idea where to find the closest hospital. Jean Paul was going in and out of consciousness as he tried to give Deon direction to L'hopital St. Charles, located in Carefour. It was a straight road to the hospital, but Tweak did not make it before they got to St. Charles hospital. By the time the doctors hooked the ivy onto Jean Paul's arm, the doctor announced that he may have lost too much blood to survive. However, Jean Paul was a fighter. The crew held vigil over Jean Paul's bed for many nights and prayed that God would spare his life.

Redemption

Marie never left Jean Paul's bedside while he was in the hospital. She helped nursed his spirit and body back to health by giving him the much needed support, love and care she felt he deserved. By the time Jean Paul left the hospital, he realized he had been given a second chance by God and a new lease on life. It was his time and calling to serve a higher purpose. He decided that he no longer wanted to be involved in the illegal activities that he was involved with in the past and wanted to change his life for the better. It was on Easter Sunday while attending church that Jean Paul and Marie decided they wanted to dedicate their lives to the Lord. They decided to make a lifetime commitment to God and their marriage. Marie also realized that she didn't have too many chances left to mess up in front of the Lord.

Jean Paul had done so much and killed so many people to get to nowhere. It was while he was laying in the hoospital while his life flashed before him that he realized that he had served no purpose in life. All the money he was trying to amass never brought him any happiness. Instead, he saw more heartache, headache and pain. He also realized that his wife loved him and he needed to put more effort into becoming a better husband. Jean Paul decided that he would turn the mansion to an orphanage for homeless children, after The Hoodfellas left.

Deon and the crew had decided they wanted to return to the States because Haiti was too much for them bear. Their initial intention was to go the island to lay back, relax and enjoy life, but that never happened. They saw more gun battle in Haiti than they had seen their whole lives in the States. Deon also wanted to bring Tweak's body back to the States with him so he could have a proper burial with his family present.

As everyone sat in the hospital mourning the loss of Tweak and Nadege, they realized how close they all came to dying as well. The Hoodfellas weren't fazed by death, but it kept knocking on their door and was inching closer to each member every single day. While everyone reminisced about the odd couple that Tweak and Nadege would have been, they also laughed at the fun memories they left behind during their time together in Haiti.

Jean Paul also learned that Reginald was the one who tipped off his brother, Groneg, about his whereabouts. Reginald was the man behind the car wreck that his wife had. He had planned the whole thing and she became a victim of his pawn. From the time his brother landed in Haiti from the States, Reginald had become a member of Antoine's gang, joining his father's old friends to wreak havoc on the rich people of Haiti. The body shop was just a front to set up his victims. Marie was one of many rich housewife victims that Reginald had set up so he could get their husbands kidnapped for a ransom. He was also behind the first kidnapping attempt on the crew when they first arrived in Haiti.

With all the trouble associated with money, Jean Paul saw no need to keep fighting for money. He tried his best to convince his friends, The Hoodfellas, to join his new path in life. They came to Haiti to find peace, but peace was not on the agenda. Going back to the States meant that they would have no choice but to deal with some unfinished business. Deon and the crew were on a different course. They had revenge on their minds when they reach the States. Somebody had to pay for the deaths of No Neck and Short Dawg, and everybody involved will pay with their life. Rosie, Evelyne and Maribel found no reason to stay in Haiti, so they decided to become part of the Hoodfellas family.

After loading up The Hoodfellas' belongings and bags of money on the cruise ship for their trip to Florida,

Jean Paul asked everyone to kneel down so he could pray for a safe trip back to the States and a prosperous life for him and his wife. It would be the last time his ship transported people illegally across the waters to the United States.

Dear Lord,

We come to you today to ask you to bless my friends Deon, Crusher, Smitty, Cindy, Evelyne, Rosie and Maribel; The Hoddfellas family. Lord, we ask you to look after them and guide them for they can only be guided by you, Lord. We also ask you to protect them from harm and to set them on a path that would guarantee their safe arrival to America, Lord.

Lord, I also pray that you change their hearts in due time and make them trust that you have your own plans for them, Lord. Lord, you are the Lord of all lords, you know that deep in their hearts they want to do right by you, please show them the light and guide their hands to the Promised Land the same way you did for me, Lord.

Thanks be to God. Let us go in peace in the name Father, the Son and the Holy Spirit.

Amen.

Hoodfellas III: Ready To Die
Coming March 2011

Sample Chapter

From
The Bedroom Bandit
By
Richard Jeanty

Chapter I
The Best Job in the World?

I'm sitting in this hospital with a broken neck, two broken arms and a broken foot wondering if I deserved what happened to me. In some way, I think I did, but I'm not completely to blame. It takes two to tangle, but my tangling ways got my ass whipped in the worst way.

A few months ago, I never saw this coming. I was deep inside Tara digging into every inch of her pussy while her husband was hard at work trying to earn a living to pay for the posh lifestyle in the suburbs that she enjoyed so much. Tara was just one of my many clients. She was the usual arm candy type of housewife that you would find in most suburbs. She was Italian and her honey complexion and sister-like shape revealed that I wasn't the only brother to ever visit her terrain. She had a nice shape, petite body type and she was as gorgeous as she wanted to be with long dark hair.

She didn't even know me from atom. All she knew was that I was there to do a job and that I was good at what I did. She teased me with her bare shoulders as she ran her fingers up and down her chest. Underneath her silk robe, was her birthday suit. A little flashing soon revealed her shaven pussy and excited clit, waiting to get licked by me.

Whatever she wanted she was going to get. Tara threw her arms around my shoulders to feel the muscular tone of my physique. She didn't talk much. She was all about action. She led me straight to the kitchen and told me, "I want you to fuck me on the counter." She had a beautiful kitchen and counter top that I could work with. I lifted her up and sat her on the counter while her feet dangled. When I spread apart her thighs, I could hear her pussy calling my name, as she instantly became moist. I felt like Lexington Steele as I bent down and started licking her inner thighs all the way up to her pussy. All I heard were her moans and groans as my tongue made contact with her pussy lips. They were a little longer than usual, like too many men had sucked on them. I proceeded to suck them lightly while sticking a finger inside her. Her pussy was dripping wet as my finger invaded her private territory. She leaned back on the counter and I attacked her perky breasts with my hands. My fingers ran circles around her erected nipples. "Fuck me already!" she screamed out.

I was more than ready to fuck her. As customary, I pulled out my extra large Magnum condom and rolled it down my thick long dick. I pulled Tara forward, toward the edge of the counter and I started fucking her. Suddenly, she wasn't so silent anymore. "Fuck me! Fuck the shit outta me!" she yelled. I was about a good eight inches in as she screamed for more. The more she screamed the more fierce my strokes became and I wanted to tear Tara's pussy up. With one finger rubbing her clit, I was fucking the hell out of Tara. Strokes after strokes after strokes, she kept begging for more. I pulled her ass forward off the counter and held on to her legs while her back rested on the counter top. My entire dick was banging her walls and Tara was on her way to heaven. "That's it. Keep fucking me," she commanded. Sweat was pouring down my body as I stroked Tara as hard as I could before she pulled her body toward me and held me while she trembled in ecstasy.

That was my usual gig and I got paid very well for doing it. I was "The Bedroom Bandit" and I was damn good at my job. My hospitalization was also the danger that came along with my job. First, you need to learn the whole story, so you can have a better understanding of my predicament.

The Bedroom Bandit
In Stores now!!!

Sample Chapters

From the book series

KWAME

By
Richard Jeanty

Chapter I

The Hero

The two men standing guard at the door didn't even see him coming. The loud thump of a punch to the throat of the six-foot-five-inch giant guarding the door with his life had the breath taken right out of him with that one punch. He stumbled to the ground without any hope of ever getting back up. His partner noticed the swift and effective delivery of the man's punch, and thought twice about approaching him. Running would be the smartest option at this time, but how cowardice would he look? The attacker was but five feet ten inches tall and perhaps one hundred and ninety pounds in weight. The security guard didn't have time on his side and before he could contemplate his next move, the attacker unloaded a kick to his groin that sent his six foot seven inch frame bowing in pain while holding his nuts for soothing comfort. Another blow to the temple followed and the man was out permanently.

At first glance, Kwame didn't stand a chance against the two giants guarding the front door. One weighed just a little less than three hundred and twenty five pounds, and the other looked like an NFL lineman at three hundred and sixty pounds. However, Kwame was a trained Navy Seal. He came home to find that the people closest to him were embroiled in a battle that threatened their livelihood daily. His sister, Candice, became a crackhead while his mother Aretha was a heroin addict. Two different types of drugs in one household, under one roof was enough to drive him crazy. Kwame didn't even recognize his sister at first. She had aged at least twice her real age and his mother was completely unrecognizable. He left her a strong woman when he joined the Navy eight years prior, but he came back to find his whole family had been under the control of drug dealers and the influence of drugs and Kwame set out to do something about it.

The two giants at the door was just the beginning of his battle to get to the low level dealers who controlled the streets where he grew up. As he made his way down the long dark corridor, he could see women with their breasts bare and fully naked, bagging the supplies of drugs for distribution throughout the community. Swift on his feet like a fast moving kitten, he was unnoticeable. He could hear the loud voices of men talking about their plans to rack up another half a million dollars from the neighborhood through their drug distribution by week's end. The strong smell of weed clouded the air as he approached the doorway to meet his nemesis. Without saying a word after setting foot in the room, he shot the first man who took notice of him right in the head. Outnumbered six to one and magazine clips sitting on the tables by the dozen and loaded weapons at reach to every person in the room, Kwame had to act fast. It was a brief stand off before the first guy reached for his Nine Millimeter automatic weapon, and just like that he found himself engulfed in a battle with flying bullets from his chest all the way down to his toes. Pandemonium broke and everybody reached for their guns at once. As Kwame rolled around on his back on the floor with a Forty Four Magnum in each hand, all five men were shot once in the head and each fell dead to the floor before they had a chance to discharge their weapons.

The naked women ran for their lives as the barrage of gunshots sent them into frenzy. The masked gun man dressed in all black was irrelevant to them. It was time to get the hell out of dodge, to a safe place away from the crackhouse. Not worried too much about the innocent women, Kwame pulled out a laundry bag and started filling it with the stack of money on the table. By the time he was done, he had estimated at least a million dollars was confiscated for the good of the community. The back door was the quickest and safest exit without being noticed. After throwing the bag of money over a wall separating the crack house from the house next door, Kwame lit his match and threw it on the gasoline that he *had poured before entering the house. The house was set ablaze and no evidence was left behind for the cops to build a case. It was one of the worse fires that Brownsville had seen in many years. No traces of human bones were left, as everything burned town to ashes by the time the New York Fire Department responded.*

Kwame had been watching the house for weeks and he intended on getting rid of everything including the people behind the big drug operation that was destroying his community. Before going to the front of the house to get rid of the security guards, he had laid out his plan to burn down the house if he couldn't get passed them. A gallon of gasoline was poured in front of all the doors except the front one where the two securities stood guard. His plan was to start the fire in the back and quickly rush to the front to pour out more gasoline to block every possible exit way, but that was his last option. His first option was to grab some of the money to begin his plans for a recreational center for the neighborhood kids. His first option worked and it was on to the next crew.

When Kwame came home he vowed to work alone to get rid of the bad elements in his neighborhood. Mad that he had to leave home to escape the belly of the beast, Kwame came back with a vengeance. He wanted to give every little boy and little girl in his neighborhood a chance at survival and a future. He understood that the military did him some good, but he had to work twice as hard to even get considered for the elite Navy Seals. The military was something that he definitely didn't want any boys from his neighborhood to join. For him it was a last resort and in the end he made the best of it. Guerilla warfare was the most precious lesson he learned while in the military and it was those tactics that he planned on using to clean up his neighborhood.

A one man show meant that only he could be the cause to his own demise. There'd be no snitches to worry about, no outside help, no betrayal and most of all no deception from anybody. Self reliance was one of the training tactics he learned in the Navy and it was time for him to apply all that he learned to make his community all it could be.

Getting rid of that crack house was one of the first priorities of his mission. Kwame knew that the crack houses were sprouting all over the neighborhood and it would take precise planning on his part to get rid of them in a timely fashion without getting caught by the police. Kwame also knew that he wasn't just going to be fighting the drug dealers, but some of the crooked cops that are part of the criminal enterprise plaguing the hood.

Due out Fall of 2011!!

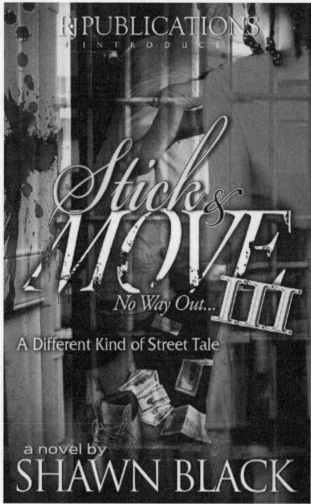

Serosa becomes the subject to information that could financially ruin and possibly destroy the lives and careers of many prominent people involved in the government if this data is exposed. As this intricate plot thickens, speculations start mounting and a whirlwind of death, deceit, and betrayal finds its way into the ranks of a once impenetrable core of the government. Will Serosa fall victim to the genetic structure that indirectly binds her to her parents causing her to realize there s NO WAY OUT!

In Stores!!!

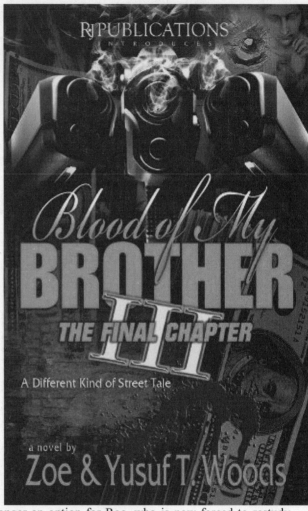

Retiring is no longer an option for Roc, who is now forced to restudy Philly's vicious streets through blood filled eyes. He realizes that his brother's killer is none other than his mentor, Mr. Holmes. With this knowledge, the strategic game of chess that began with the pushing of a pawn in the Blood of My Brother series, symbolizes one of love, loyalty, blood, mayhem, and death. In the end, the streets of Philadelphia will never be the same...

In Storess!!!

After Chasin' Satisfaction, Julius finds that satisfaction is not all that it's cracked up to be. It left nothing but death in its aftermath. Now living the glamorous life in Miami while putting the finishing touches on his hybrid condo hotel, he realizes with newfound success he's now become the hunted. Julian's success is threatened as someone from his past vows revenge on him.

In Stores!!!

It may not be Histeria Lane, but these desperate housewives are fed up with their neglecting husbands. Their sexual needs take precedence over the millions of dollars their husbands bring home every year to keep them happy in their affluent neighborhood. While their husbands claim to be hard at work, these wives are doing a little work of their own with the bedroom bandit. Is the bandit swift enough to evade these angry husbands?

In Stores!!

NEGLECTED SOULS

Motherhood and the trials of loving too hard and not enough frame this story...The realism of these characters will bring tears to your spirit as you discover the hero in the villain you never saw coming...

In Stores!!!

Jimmy and Nina continue to feel a void in their lives because they haven't a clue about their genealogical make-up. Jimmy falls victims to a life threatening illness and only the right organ donor can save his life. Will the donor be the bridge to reconnect Jimmy and Nina to their biological family? Will Nina be the strength for her brother in his time of need? Will they ever find out what really happened to their mother?

In Stores!!!

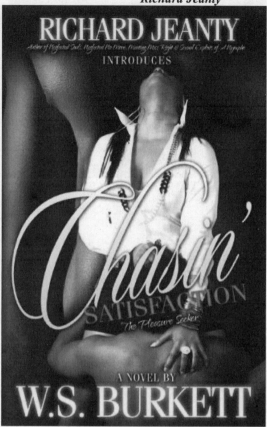

Betrayal, lust, lies, murder, deception, sex and tainted love frame this story... Julian Stevens lacks the ambition and freak ability that Miko looks for in a man, but she married him despite his flaws to spite an ex-boyfriend. When Miko least expects it, the old boyfriend shows up and ready to sweep her off her feet again. She wants to have her cake and eat it too. While Miko's doing her own thing, Julian is determined to become everything Miko ever wanted in a man and more, but will he go to extreme lengths to prove he's worthy of Miko's love? Julian Stevens soon finds out that he's capable of being more than he could ever imagine as he embarks on a journey that will change his life forever.

In Stores!!!

The police in New York and other major cities around the country are increasingly victimizing black men. The violence has escalated to deadly force, most of the time without justification. In this controversial book, noted author Richard Jeanty, tackles the problem of police brutality and the unfair treatment of Black men at the hands of police in New York City and the rest of the country.

In Stores!!!

Just when Darren thinks his relationship with Tina is flourishing, there is yet another hurdle on the road hindering their bliss. Tina saw a therapist for months to deal with her sexual addiction, but now Darren is wondering if she was ever treated completely. Darren has not been taking care of home and Tina's frustrated and agrees to a break-up with Darren. Will Darren lose Tina for good? Will Tina ever realize that Darren is the best man for her?

In Stores!!

Ronald Murphy was a player all his life until he and his best friend, Myles, met the women of their dreams during a brief vacation in South Beach, Florida. Sexual Jeopardy is story of trust, betrayal, forgiveness, friendship and hope.

In Stores!!!

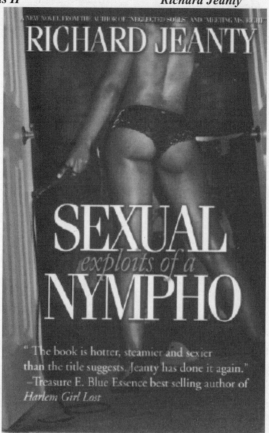

Tina develops an insatiable sexual appetite very early in life. She
only loves her boyfriend, Darren, but he's too far away in college to satisfy her sexual needs.
Tina decides to get buck wild away in college
Will her sexual trysts jeopardize the lives of the men in her life?

In Stores!!!

Faith Jones, a woman in her mid-thirties, has given up on ever finding love again until she met her son's best friend, Darius. Faith Jones is walking a thin line of betrayal against her son for the love of Darius. Will Faith allow her emotions to outweigh her common sense?

In Stores!!!

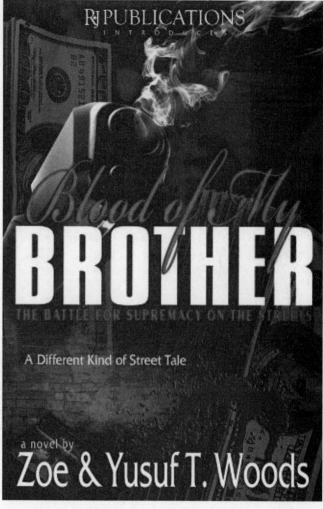

Roc was the man on the streets of Philadelphia, until his younger brother decided it was time to become his own man by wreaking havoc on Roc's crew without any regards for the blood relation they share. Drug, murder, mayhem and the pursuit of happiness can lead to deadly consequences. This story can only be told by a person who has lived it.

In Stores!!!

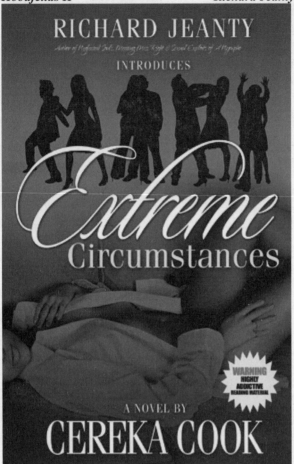

What happens when a devoted woman is betrayed? Come take a ride with Chanel as she takes her boyfriend, Donnell, to circumstances beyond belief after he betrays her trust with his endless infidelities. How long can Chanel's friend, Janai, use her looks to get what she wants from men before it catches up to her? Find out as Janai's gold-digging ways catch up with and she has to face the consequences of her extreme actions.

In Stores!!!

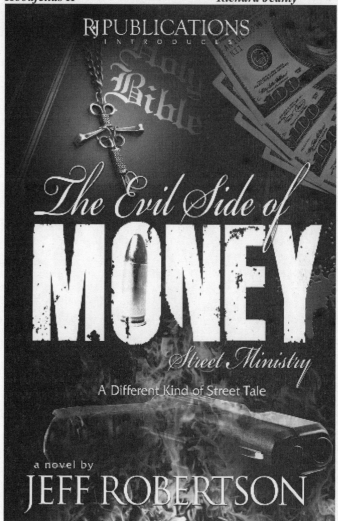

Violence, Intimidation and carnage are the order as Nathan and his brother set out to build the most powerful drug empires in Chicago. However, when God comes knocking, Nathan's conscience starts to surface. Will his haunted criminal past get the best of him?

In Stores!!

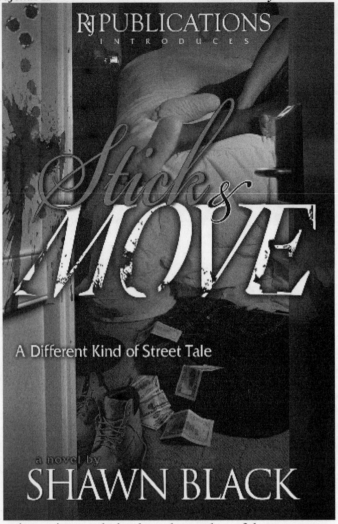

RJ PUBLICATIONS
INTRODUCES

Stick & MOVE

A Different Kind of Street Tale

a novel by
SHAWN BLACK

Yasmina witnessed the brutal murder of her parents at a young age at the hand of a drug dealer. This event stained her mind and upbringing as a result. Will Yamina's life come full circle with her past? Find out as Yasmina's crew, The Platinum Chicks, set out to make a name for themselves on the street.

In stores!!

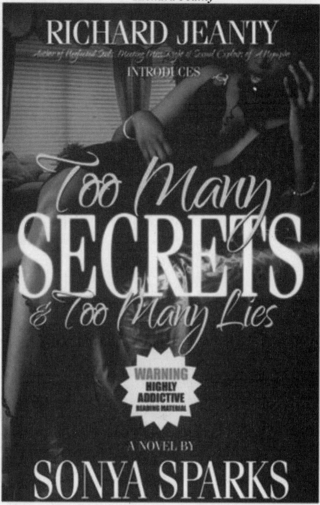

RICHARD JEANTY

Author of Neglected Souls, Meeting Mrs. Right & Sexual Exploits of A Nympho

INTRODUCES

Too Many

SECRETS

& Too Many Lies

WARNING
**HIGHLY
ADDICTIVE**
READING MATERIAL

A NOVEL BY

SONYA SPARKS

Ashland's mother, Bianca, fights hard to suppress the truth from her daughter because she doesn't want her to marry Jordan, the grandson of an ex-lover she loathes. Ashland soon finds out how cruel and vengeful her mother can be, but what price will Bianca pay for redemption?

In stores!!

Malcolm is a wealthy virgin who decides to conceal his wealth From the world until he meets the right woman. His wealthy best friend, Dexter, hides his wealth from no one. Malcolm struggles to find love in an environment where vanity and materialism are rampant, while Dexter is getting more than enough of his share of women. Malcolm needs develop self-esteem and confidence to meet the right woman and Dexter's confidence is borderline arrogance.
Will bad boys like Dexter continue to take women for a ride?

Or will nice guys like Malcolm continue to finish last?

In Stores!!!

What happens when a woman's devotion to her fiancee is tested weeks before she gets married? What if her fiancee is just hiding behind the veil of ministry to deceive her? Find out as Sean Mitchell takes you on a journey you'll never forget into the lives of Angelica, Titus and Aurelius.

In Stores!!

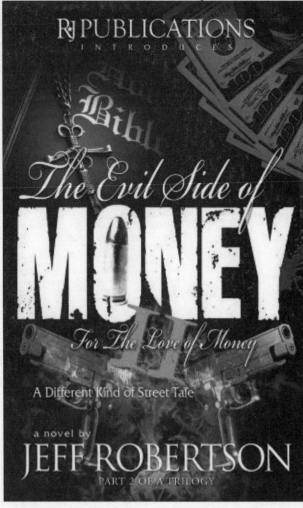

A beautigul woman from Bolivia threatens the existence of the drug empire that Nate and G have built. While Nate is head over heels for her, G can see right through her. As she brings on more conflict between the crew, G sets out to show Nate exactly who she is before she brings about their demise.

In Stores!!!

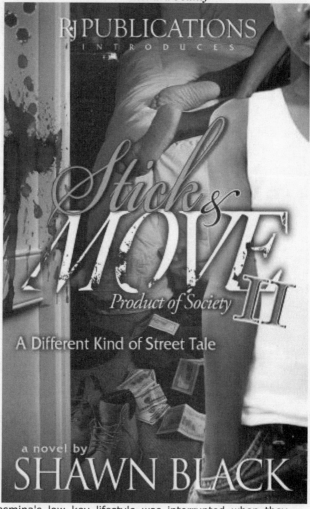

Scorcher and Yasmina's low key lifestyle was interrupted when they were taken down by the Feds, but their daughter, Serosa, was left to be raised by the foster care system. Will Serosa become a product of her environment or will she rise above it all? Her bloodline is undeniable, but will she be able to control it?

In Stores!!

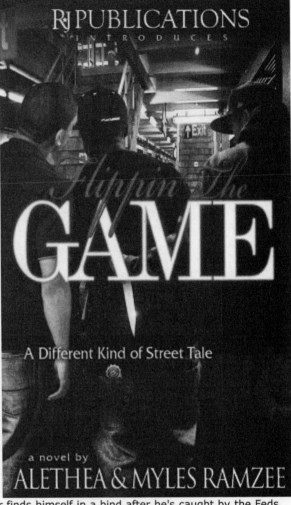

An ex-drug dealer finds himself in a bind after he's caught by the Feds. He has to decide which is more important, his family or his loyalty to the game. As he fights hard to make a decision, those who helped him to the top fear the worse from him. Will he get the chance to tell the govt. whole story, or will someone get to him before he becomes a snitch?

In Stores!!!

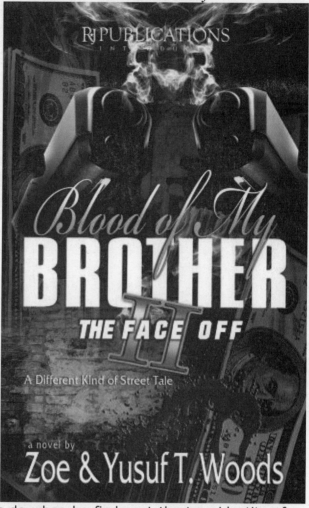

What will Roc do when he finds out the true identity of Solo? Will the blood shed come from his own brother Lil Mac? Will Roc and Solo take their beef to an explosive height on the street? Find out as Zoe and Yusuf bring the second installment to their hot street joint, Blood of My Brother.

In Stores!!!

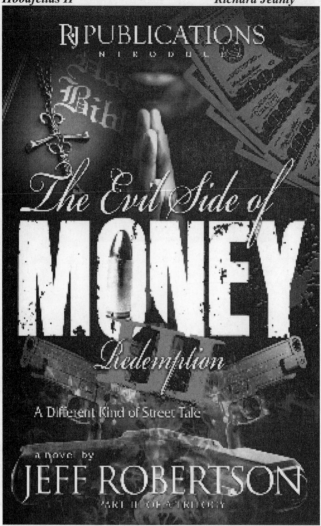

Forced to abandon the drug world for good, Nathan and G
attempt to change their lives and move forward, but will
their past come back to haunt them? This final installment
will leave you speechless.

In Stores!!!

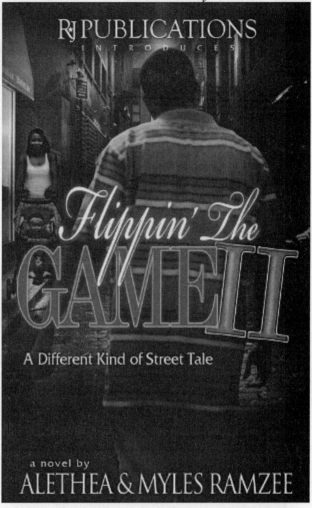

Nafiys Muhammad managed to beat the charges in court and was found innocent as a result. However, his criminal involvement is far from over. While Jerry Class Classon is feeling safe in the witness protection program, his family continues to endure even more pain. There will be many revelations as betrayal, sex scandal, corruption, and murder shape this story. No one will be left unscathed and everyone will pay the price for his/her involvement. Get ready for a rough ride as we revisit the Black Top Crew.

In Stores!!

Dave Richardson is enjoying success as his second book became a New York Times best-seller. He left the life of The Bedroom behind to settle with his family, but an obsessed fan has not had enough of Dave and she will go to great length to get a piece of him. How far will a woman go to get a man that doesn't belong to her?

Coming September 2010

Deon is at the mercy of a ruthless gang that kidnapped him. In a foreign land where he knows nothing about the culture, he has to use his survival instincts and his wit to outsmart his captors. Will the Hoodfellas show up in time to rescue Deon, or will Crazy D take over once again and fight an all out war by himself?

Coming March 2010

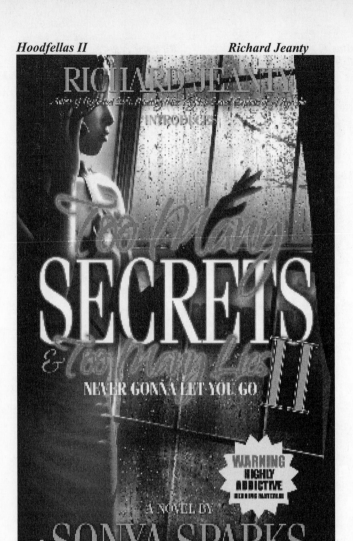

The drama continues as Deshun is hunted by Angela who still feels that ex-girlfriend Kayla is still trying to win his heart, though he brutally raped her. Angela will kill anyone who gets in her way, but is DeShun worth all the aggravation?

In Stores!!!

RICHARD JEANTY

Author of *Neglected Souls* and *Neglected No More*

Ignorant SOULS

THE FINAL EPISODE TO THE NEGLECTED SOULS SERIES

Buck Johnson was forced to make the best out of worst situation. He has witnessed the most cruel events in his life and it is those events who the man that he has become. Was the Johnson family ignorant souls through no fault of their own?

In Stores!!!

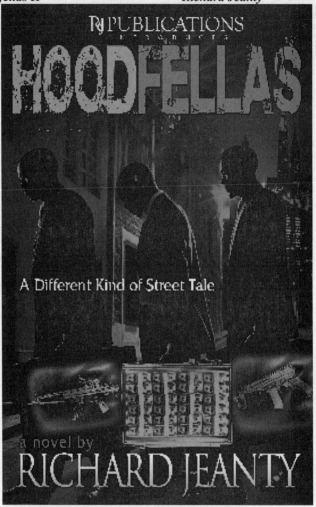

When an Ex-con finds himself destitute and in dire need of the basic necessities after he's released from prison, he turns to what he knows best, crime, but at what cost? Extortion, murder and mayhem drives him back to the top, but will he stay there?

In Stores !!!

What happens when someone falls insanely in love?
Stalking is just the beginning.
In Stores!!!

Use this coupon to order by mail

1. Neglected Souls, Richard Jeanty $14.95 Available
2. Neglected No More, Richard Jeanty $14.95 Available
3. Ignorant Souls, Richard Jeanty $15.00, Available
4. Sexual Exploits of Nympho, Richard Jeanty $14.95 Available
5. Meeting Ms. Right's Whip Appeal, Richard Jeanty $14.95 Available
6. Me and Mrs. Jones, K.M Thompson $14.95 Available
7. Chasin' Satisfaction, W.S Burkett $14.95 Available
8. Extreme Circumstances, Cereka Cook $14.95 Available
9. The Most Dangerous Gang In America, R. Jeanty $15.00 Available
10. Sexual Exploits of a Nympho II, Richard Jeanty $15.00 Available
11. Sexual Jeopardy, Richard Jeanty $14.95 Available
12. Too Many Secrets, Too Many Lies, Sonya Sparks $15.00 Available
13. Stick And Move, Shawn Black $15.00 Available
14. Evil Side Of Money, Jeff Robertson $15.00 Available
15. Evil Side Of Money II, Jeff Robertson $15.00 Available
16. Evil Side Of Money III, Jeff Robertson $15.00 Available
17. Flippin' The Game, Alethea and M. Ramzee, $15.00 Available
18. Flippin' The Game II, Alethea and M. Ramzee, $15.00 Available
19. Cater To Her, W.S Burkett $15.00 Available
20. Blood of My Brother I, Zoe & Yusuf Woods $15.00 Available
21. Blood of my Brother II, Zoe & Ysuf Woods $15.00 Available
22. Hoodfellas, Richard Jeanty $15.00 available
23. Hoodfellas II, Richard Jeanty, $15.00 03/30/2010
24. The Bedroom Bandit, Richard Jeanty $15.00 Available
25. Mr. Erotica, Richard Jeanty, $15.00, Sept 2010
26. Stick N Move II, Shawn Black $15.00 Available
27. Stick N Move III, Shawn Black $15.00 Available
28. Miami Noire, W.S. Burkett $15.00 Available
29. Insanely In Love, Cereka Cook $15.00 Available
30. Blood of My Brother III, Zoe & Yusuf Woods Available

Name_____
Address_____
City_____State_____Zip Code_____

Please send the novels that I have circled above.
Shipping and Handling: Free
Total Number of Books_____
Total Amount Due_____

Buy 3 books and get 1 free. This offer is subject to change without notice.
Send institution check or money order (no cash or CODs) to:
RJ Publications
PO Box 300771
Jamaica, NY 11434
For more information please call 718-471-2926, or visit www.rjpublications.com

Please allow 2-3 weeks for delivery.

Use this coupon to order by mail
31. Neglected Souls, Richard Jeanty $14.95 Available
32. Neglected No More, Richard Jeanty $14.95 Available
33. Ignorant Souls, Richard Jeanty $15.00, Available
34. Sexual Exploits of Nympho, Richard Jeanty $14.95 Available
35. Meeting Ms. Right's Whip Appeal, Richard Jeanty $14.95 Available
36. Me and Mrs. Jones, K.M Thompson $14.95 Available
37. Chasin' Satisfaction, W.S Burkett $14.95 Available
38. Extreme Circumstances, Cereka Cook $14.95 Available
39. The Most Dangerous Gang In America, R. Jeanty $15.00 Available
40. Sexual Exploits of a Nympho II, Richard Jeanty $15.00 Available
41. Sexual Jeopardy, Richard Jeanty $14.95 Available
42. Too Many Secrets, Too Many Lies, Sonya Sparks $15.00 Available
43. Stick And Move, Shawn Black $15.00 Available
44. Evil Side Of Money, Jeff Robertson $15.00 Available
45. Evil Side Of Money II, Jeff Robertson $15.00 Available
46. Evil Side Of Money III, Jeff Robertson $15.00 Available
47. Flippin' The Game, Alethea and M. Ramzee, $15.00 Available
48. Flippin' The Game II, Alethea and M. Ramzee, $15.00 Available
49. Cater To Her, W.S Burkett $15.00 Available
50. Blood of My Brother I, Zoe & Yusuf Woods $15.00 Available
51. Blood of my Brother II, Zoe & Ysuf Woods $15.00 Available
52. Hoodfellas, Richard Jeanty $15.00 available
53. Hoodfellas II, Richard Jeanty, $15.00 03/30/2010
54. The Bedroom Bandit, Richard Jeanty $15.00 Available
55. Mr. Erotica, Richard Jeanty, $15.00, Sept 2010
56. Stick N Move II, Shawn Black $15.00 Available
57. Stick N Move III, Shawn Black $15.00 Available
58. Miami Noire, W.S. Burkett $15.00 Available
59. Insanely In Love, Cereka Cook $15.00 Available
60. Blood of My Brother III, Zoe & Yusuf Woods Available

Name_____
Address_____
City_____State_____Zip Code_____

Please send the novels that I have circled above.
Shipping and Handling: Free
Total Number of Books_____
Total Amount Due_____
Buy 3 books and get 1 free. This offer is subject to change without notice.
Send institution check or money order (no cash or CODs) to:
RJ Publications
PO Box 300771
Jamaica, NY 11434
For more information please call 718-471-2926, or visit www.rjpublications.com

Please allow 2-3 weeks for delivery.

PUBLICATIONS
BRINGING EXCITEMENT, FUN AND JOY TO READING

Use this coupon to order by mail

61. Neglected Souls, Richard Jeanty $14.95 Available
62. Neglected No More, Richard Jeanty $14.95 Available
63. Ignorant Souls, Richard Jeanty $15.00, Available
64. Sexual Exploits of Nympho, Richard Jeanty $14.95 Available
65. Meeting Ms. Right's Whip Appeal, Richard Jeanty $14.95 Available
66. Me and Mrs. Jones, K.M Thompson $14.95 Available
67. Chasin' Satisfaction, W.S Burkett $14.95 Available
68. Extreme Circumstances, Cereka Cook $14.95 Available
69. The Most Dangerous Gang In America, R. Jeanty $15.00 Available
70. Sexual Exploits of a Nympho II, Richard Jeanty $15.00 Available
71. Sexual Jeopardy, Richard Jeanty $14.95 Available
72. Too Many Secrets, Too Many Lies, Sonya Sparks $15.00 Available
73. Stick And Move, Shawn Black $15.00 Available
74. Evil Side Of Money, Jeff Robertson $15.00 Available
75. Evil Side Of Money II, Jeff Robertson $15.00 Available
76. Evil Side Of Money III, Jeff Robertson $15.00 Available
77. Flippin' The Game, Alethea and M. Ramzee, $15.00 Available
78. Flippin' The Game II, Alethea and M. Ramzee, $15.00 Available
79. Cater To Her, W.S Burkett $15.00 Available
80. Blood of My Brother I, Zoe & Yusuf Woods $15.00 Available
81. Blood of my Brother II, Zoe & Ysuf Woods $15.00 Available
82. Hoodfellas, Richard Jeanty $15.00 available
83. Hoodfellas II, Richard Jeanty, $15.00 03/30/2010
84. The Bedroom Bandit, Richard Jeanty $15.00 Available
85. Mr. Erotica, Richard Jeanty, $15.00, Sept 2010
86. Stick N Move II, Shawn Black $15.00 Available
87. Stick N Move III, Shawn Black $15.00 Available
88. Miami Noire, W.S. Burkett $15.00 Available
89. Insanely In Love, Cereka Cook $15.00 Available
90. Blood of My Brother III, Zoe & Yusuf Woods Available

Name_____

Address_____

City_____State_____Zip Code_____

Please send the novels that I have circled above.
Shipping and Handling: Free
Total Number of Books_____
Total Amount Due_____
Buy 3 books and get 1 free. This offer is subject to change without notice.
Send institution check or money order (no cash or CODs) to:
RJ Publications
PO Box 300771
Jamaica, NY 11434
For more information please call 718-471-2926, or visit www.rjpublications.com

Please allow 2-3 weeks for delivery